BIG HORSE, LITTLE HORSE

By MARTHA GOLDBERG

Pictures by JOE LASKER

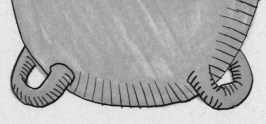

SCHOLASTIC BOOK SERVICES

NEW YORK • TORONTO • LONDON • AUCKLAND • SYDNEY

for Ethel

This edition has been especially edited for Lucky Book Club Readers.

Copyright © 1960 by Martha Goldberg. Copyright © 1963 by Scholastic Magazines, Inc. This
edition is published by Scholastic Book Services, a division of Scholastic Magazines, Inc., by
arrangement with The Macmillan Co.
6th printing .... April 1970

Printed in the U.S.A.

This story is about a Mexican boy named Mateo. You know, of course, that in Mexico everyone speaks Spanish. Here are some Spanish words you will find in this book:

Si means *yes*.

Si, Señor means *yes, sir*.

Adios means *good-by*.

Plaza is an open place in the center of the village.

Tortillas are Mexican bread. They look like pancakes.

Olla is a large jar. It is used to carry water.

Mateo's family are potters. They make pots and toys out of clay. Here are some words that have to do with making pottery:

A kiln is a small oven for baking clay pottery. The pottery is not ready until it is baked.

To **fire** a pot means to bake it in a kiln.

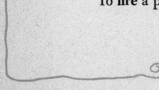

Early one morning, Mateo led his burro down the mountain. The little burro was almost buried under a heavy load of firewood. It stopped to rest on the trail.

"Get up, slow one. Mama is waiting for the wood," Mateo said. He tapped the burro lightly with a stick.

Far below were the red tile roofs of Mateo's village. There each family made the black pottery which was famous all over Mexico.

Mateo's mother was one of the finest potters of the village. Today she would fire the *ollas* — the large water jars. So Mateo hurried with the wood.

For still another reason he hurried. He wanted to see the beautiful brown horse, Panchita, who belonged to Big Pablo.

On his way from the mountain he had often stopped to watch her. He had even tried to model a clay horse. But his horses had never looked like Panchita. Mateo wanted to see her again before he tried to make another clay horse.

Mateo was sure that he could make a good clay horse. This was a secret that no one knew.

Not even his sister, Concha, knew the secret.

Someday, he said to himself, he would become a fine potter like his mother.

At the edge of the village the trail became a wide, dusty road. Then Mateo went more

quickly. Near Big Pablo's home, the horse
Panchita was out in the field. She ran in wide,
joyful circles. She rolled over and rubbed her
back on the ground. She kicked her heels in
the air like a colt. Mateo laughed to see her.

Now he could see why his little clay horse
had not looked like Panchita. He had given it

long ears like a *burrito!* Panchita's ears were small. Her mane and tail were long and silky. "When I get home," Mateo thought, "I will know how to make a clay horse that looks like her."

Big Pablo came to him as he stood watching Panchita.

"Good day, *Señor*," Mateo called out.

"Good day, Mateo," Big Pablo answered. "Look well at Panchita, for soon she will be gone. I will take her to the Saturday Market."

Mateo was shocked. "You will sell Panchita!" he said. "What a pity."

How could anyone want to sell so fine a horse? "Panchita is worth many *burritos*," he said to Big Pablo. "She is big and strong, and she runs very fast."

"That is true," Big Pablo answered. "But also Panchita eats much. I must sell her. May the Almighty One grant her a good home."

Mateo turned away. He was too sad to speak. He drove the burro slowly along the road. If Panchita left the village, he would never see her again. She must not leave!

Then Mateo had an idea. His family could use a horse. He would ask his father to buy her.

When Mateo reached home, his father called out, "Mama is waiting for the wood. Where have you been so long?"

"I stopped at Big Pablo's," Mateo answered.

"You stopped while we waited for you?" his father asked.

"*Si*," Mateo said, all in a rush. "Big Pablo is selling Panchita. Please, Papa, can we not buy her?"

"Do you know why Big Pablo sells her, little son?" his father asked.

"*Si*, Papa," Mateo said.

"Are we so rich, then, that I should buy a

horse? Should I buy a horse because my son has set his heart on it? A horse, ha! Next you will be asking that I buy a motorcar. Go and unload the wood, foolish one. Let me hear no more about Panchita."

Mateo said nothing. He led the burro to the woodpile. Quickly he took the wood off the burro's back and put it on the woodpile. Then he took the burro to his father. His father was going back to the mountain for some more firewood.

After his father left, Mateo went into the
house for a lump of the grayish-brown clay.
He came back to the woodpile and sat down
on the ground behind it. Now no one would
see him.

Mateo began to work quickly with the clay.
First he rolled it into a ball. Then he wet his

fingers in a bowl of muddy water and smoothed the ball of clay. He pinched one end to make the head and the tiny ears. Then he made the legs and tail out of the small rolls of clay.

He held up the little horse to look at it. It was not right. A horse was harder to make than a clay whistle in the shape of a bird. A horse was harder to make than an angel whose wide skirt was really a bell. These things his mother had taught him to make. But he knew he could make his horse now. Would he have time to make it before someone found his hiding place?

He bent the soft clay legs. Now his little horse began to look like the big horse Panchita running across the field. As he worked, he thought of the answers he might have given his father: A horse would make quick work of plowing the cornfield. A horse could carry the pottery to market in large bags hung over her sides. He and Concha and Baby Rosita could all ride on her, too. Could a burro carry so much?

But there was one big question he could not answer: What would they feed Panchita?

"Mateo! Mateo!" It was his sister Concha calling him.

Mateo pushed himself still closer to the house.

Concha soon grew tired of looking for him. Her voice faded away. Now all was quiet as Mateo worked. He drew with his fingernail to make the horse's mane. He used a tiny stick to mark the eyes and nose. Then with wet fingers he smoothed over the little clay body again.

"Mateo! You are there! Come here!"

It was Mama calling him this time. She was angry.

Mateo knew he must answer her. He covered the clay horse with his hand. Then he walked into the *patio*.

"I am here, *Mamacita*," he said.

"Why did you not come when I sent Concha for you?" his mother asked.

Mateo held out the horse for her to see. "I was making this," he said. "I wanted to finish it."

Mama took the little horse gently into her hands.

"It is good," she said in a surprised voice.

"May I fire it?" Mateo asked eagerly.

"If you wish," Mama said, "but it is very small and thin. It may break in the firing."

"Then I shall make a larger one," Mateo said quickly.

"No, my son," his mother shook her head. "You must make the toys that we can sell. No one buys clay horses."

Mateo turned his head away to hide the tears in his eyes. Not to make a little horse like Panchita! Soon she would be gone forever. It was almost too much to bear.

His mother did not seem to notice how Mateo felt. She went on talking "Mateo, your grandmother has a fever. I must take food to her. There is work for you to do while I am gone."

"Do you wish me to watch the fire?"

"I could not fire the water jars this morning," his mother said. "You came too late with the wood."

"I watched Panchita for a little while," Mateo explained.

"Always you watch Panchita," his mother said. "Will you never learn to come when we are waiting for you?"

Mateo hung his head and said in a low voice, "I am ashamed, Mama."

"Do not do it again, little son," his mother said. She went quickly into the house and brought out a large basket. She placed the basket on a table against the *patio* wall.

Then Mateo's mother saw his sad face. She put her hand on Mateo's shoulder and said with a smile, "It is well that there is no fire to watch. I must go away today."

"I will go with you to grandmother's house," Mateo said.

"No, son," his mother said. "Rafael is bringing the tourists to see how the black pottery is made. You and Concha must be ready. You must help me."

Mama and Papa had good reason to be angry with him this morning, Mateo thought. But he would show them that he could do his work well. Then maybe Mama would let him make a clay horse some other day.

"Concha and I will do as you wish, *Mamacita*," he said. "When will you return?"

"By the next bus," his mother said. She moved quickly as she spoke.

Mateo went after her, watching as she took *tortillas*, beans, and chicken for grandmother and placed them in the basket. She covered the food with a clean cloth.

Then she said, "You must sweep the *patio* and set out the chairs. Also, you must have the clay ready. Cover it well with a wet cloth."

Mateo nodded.

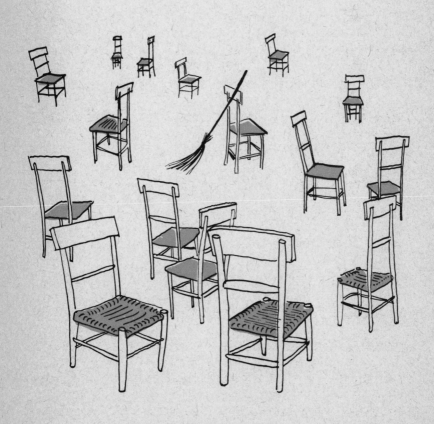

"Put out a large *olla* — one that is almost dry. I will decorate it as the tourists watch," his mother added. "And on the big table put the toys and bowls we have made to sell."

"*Si*," Mateo said. "Concha and I will polish them well."

"Take care that you do all that I have told you to do," his mother said.

"Do not worry, *Mamacita*," Mateo answered.

Just then Concha ran into the yard. She called, "*Mamacita! Mamacita!* The bus! The bus is coming."

"I will go now," Mama said.

She tied Baby Rosita tightly in her shawl. Then she placed a roll of cloth like a crown on the top of her head. On this she set the basket of food.

"*Adios!* Till we meet again," she said as she started down the road.

"*Adios, Mamacita!*" Mateo and Concha answered. "Go with God."

Turning around, Mama called back, "Mateo, if it rains you must carry in the firewood and the jars that are drying in the sun."

"I will remember," Mateo called after her.

Concha took a broom and began to sweep the *patio*. Mateo wet the ground to settle the dust.

Next, he and Concha carried the chairs into the patio. They put them in a circle. Each chair faced the mat where Mama would sit later to work the clay.

They cleaned off the big table and brought out the basket of small toys. They polished the toys with a soft cloth until the whistles and bells and little dishes made of black pottery shone in the bright sunshine.

Mama would be pleased.

"Concha," Mateo said, "go to the *plaza* and wait for the bus. Carry the baby so that Mama may come quickly."

After Concha had gone, Mateo squatted on the ground. How his fingers wanted to make another clay horse — a clay horse that would

remind him of Panchita. If only Mama would
let him make such a horse!

As he waited, a few drops of rain fell. Then
all at once the rain poured down. It was like
a solid wall of water.

Mateo jumped up. He must carry in the firewood. It should be dry when Mama made a fire
in the kiln. He would get the *ollas* later.

He ran to the woodpile and picked up an
armload of branches. He held them against his
body. They tickled and scratched him as he
ran. Mateo dropped the branches on the dry
ground under the roof of the open shed. Then
he ran back for more.

He came to the opening in the cactus fence and went quickly out to the road. "Concha! Concha!" he called. But he did not wait to see if she would come.

Mateo ran back to the woodpile. He filled his arms with branches again. His clothes dripped with water. His bare feet were covered with mud. Back and forth he ran.

The rain poured down, making puddles in the yard. Mateo saw that the clay *ollas* were standing in water. Should he stop and put them away before they were spoiled? But what good were clay jars without dry firewood?

"Concha! Concha!" he shouted again in his loudest voice. But he was afraid she would not hear him above the noise of the rain.

Only one armload of wood was left. As Mateo turned to get it, Concha ran in from the road.

Breathless, she picked up two of the large jars. She turned each one over and shook the water from it. She ran with the jars to the house and set them down on the dirt floor.

Mateo went to help her. She was ahead of him. He picked up two jars. Racing after her, he called, "Who will get there first?"

Mateo did not see the little pig that was running across the yard. He tripped over the

pig and fell down. The jars broke into pieces. The pig ran away squealing. Mateo was left on the ground with broken pottery all around him.

Concha was laughing. Mateo got up. He brushed the mud and bits of broken pottery from his hands and clothes. His face was very sad. Again he had done something wrong!

"They were fine big *ollas*," he said sadly. "And I cannot make others for Mama. She will be angry with me."

"But I will tell Mama that the little pig tripped you," Concha told him.

She helped Mateo carry all the big jars into the house. Then Concha and Mateo stood in the open doorway and watched the rain. After a little while, Mateo went out into the yard again to see if they had forgotten anything.

Every stick of firewood and all the *ollas* were under cover. He let out his breath in relief.

Mateo walked back to Concha and said, "You came from the *plaza* just in time."

The *plaza!* The bus! In his hurry Mateo had forgotten it.

"Did not the bus come?" he asked.

Concha shook her head. "They say it has stopped on the bridge."

"The tourists will come soon," Mateo said, "and Mama is not here."

"*Mamacita* will walk," Concha said.

"*Si,*" answered Mateo, "but the tourists in cars will come first."

The rain stopped just as quickly as it had started. The sun shone again in a bright blue sky. The chairs were drying. The water was soaking into the ground.

Concha and Mateo heard the sound of cars in the road. They heard car doors slamming. They heard people talking. The tourists were here! Rafael, the guide, led the tourists into the *patio.*

Mateo ran to Rafael and drew him aside. "All is ready," he whispered, "but Mama is not here. This morning she went to see my grandmother, and she has not come back."

"Do not worry," Rafael said. "I shall show the kiln and the clay. I will also show the clay things your mother has made. She will come soon."

Mateo felt better then. He turned to Concha and said, "Go back to the *plaza* and wait for Mama."

Concha left the *patio* quickly.

The tourists were looking at the small toys on the table. Mateo stood near them. He did not understand their words. But he could tell that they liked the fine toys. He was proud. He and Concha had made these toys. If the little clay horse were here on the table, would the tourists like it too, Mateo wondered.

Rafael called everyone together in the *patio*. He told them how Papa had dug the clay from the bank of the river and cleaned out all the sand and rocks. He told how Mama and Papa wet the dry clay and worked it with their hands until it was soft and ready to use.

Then Rafael took the tourists into the house and showed them the *ollas* — the water jars. He pointed out the other clay things — the cooking pots and baking dishes and the bowls.

"Now," Rafael said, "we will go into the yard and see the kiln where the pottery is fired. Only the potters of this village know the secret of making black pottery."

Papa had dug a deep hole in the ground to make the kiln. Near the bottom he had made a row of bricks. Rafael showed the tourists how Mama put the clay pieces on the row of bricks. He showed them how she covered the clay with bits of broken pottery. He showed them the place underneath the bricks where Mama made the fire. He told them how Mama closed the kiln with earth.

Now it was time for Mama to sit on the straw mat to make an olla. This was the most important part of the visit. But Mama was not here! The tourists had gone back into the *patio*. They were sitting in the chairs. What should Mateo and Rafael do?

Mateo ran to the fence and looked down the road. There he saw people still waiting for the bus. But the bus was on the bridge and would not move.

If Papa were here, he would take Mama's place on the mat and make an *olla*. But it was

many hours before Papa would come back from the mountains. Mama had asked *him*, *Mateo*, to help with the tourists. He must do what he could.

Mateo walked back into the patio and said to Rafael in a low voice, "I can decorate an *olla*. Perhaps Mama will come while I work on the *olla*."

Rafael spoke to the people seated in the chairs. "Today, Mateo will decorate an *olla*. He is only eight years old, but he is already a good potter."

Mateo had brought a large *olla* from the house. It had been drying for several days, but had not been fired. With a sharp, thin piece of stone, he made fine lines around the neck of the jar. Then, on the widest part of the jar, he drew a large flower with a stem and leaves.

He held the *olla* up to show what he had
done. Then he turned the stone over and used
the smooth, flat side to polish the jar. He

stopped and held it up again. It was beautiful.
He set it down, for it was ready to be fired.

Mateo had worked as long as he could. He had hoped that Mama would come. Now he was finished, and she was not here.

Some of the tourists stood up and began to move about the *patio*. Soon they would go away. They would not see how the black pottery was made.

If only Mama would come, Mateo thought.

He stood up and ran quickly out to the road again. Down near the *plaza* someone was walking. But Mateo could see that it was not Mama. It was a man with a horse. It was Big Pablo taking Panchita away from the village!

A tear ran down Mateo's cheek. "*Adios*, Panchita," he said softly. "Go with God."

Everything has gone wrong today, Mateo thought. He turned and walked slowly back toward the *patio*. Panchita was on her way to market. The tourists were leaving. He had not been able to show them how Mama made the black pottery.

He reached the patio. The tourists were still there. If only he could make an *olla!* But Mama had said that he was too small to work with the large jars. And if he made a little toy whistle or a bell, no one would be able to see.

But he could make a horse like the beautiful Panchita! Today Mama had said that his little horse was good. Should he make a bigger one while the people watched?

He had done so many things wrong today. Mama had told him not to make a bigger horse, but it was the only thing he could do. When Mama came back, he would explain. Only sometimes she did not listen, but punished quickly, he thought.

Mateo sat down on the mat and picked up a ball of the wet clay. Quickly he shaped the round body, the small head, and the tiny ears.

The people began to watch him work. Those who had been standing sat down.

He made the neck with the mane flying in the wind. He formed the legs with rolls of clay. He made the tail with another roll. How like Panchita the little horse was beginning to look!

Mateo held up his work and smiled. The people smiled back. And then Mateo saw his mother. She stood behind the row of chairs with Rafael and Concha. She had been watching as he worked with the clay!

Mateo's fingers grew stiff. The little horse was again just a lump of cold, wet clay in his hands. He wanted to drop it and run away. His

mother was a fine potter. Some said she was the finest potter in all of Mexico. He could not work as she watched. It was *she* who should be here on the mat — not Mateo.

Mateo put the horse down. He waited for his mother to come and take his place. She shook her head. Mateo thought that she did not understand. He stood up and walked toward her. But she shook her head again and pointed to the mat.

Mateo went back to the mat and sat down. Slowly he picked up the little clay horse. Mama wanted him to finish! He could hardly believe it. But she was smiling and waiting for him to go on.

He picked up a sharp stick and drew the eyes. His fingernail made the fine lines on the mane and tail to look like hair. Mateo wet his fingers in the bowl of water and smoothed over the little body. He was finished.

He looked up at his mother.

She came to him, and Mateo said quickly, "I could not make an *olla* like yours, *Mamacita*. I made the big horse like Panchita because I could make nothing else."

"You did well, Mateo," his mother answered. She took the clay horse from him. She turned it over carefully. "It is well made, little son," she said. "It will fire well."

Those were the finest words Mama could say. Mateo was filled with happiness.

The people had left their chairs and were talking to Rafael.

"Many of the tourists would like to buy the horse when it is fired," Rafael said to Mateo. "Will you make others?"

"I do not know," Mateo said. He looked at his mother.

She smiled at him and nodded.

"*Si*," Mateo said proudly. "I will make many more."

Yes, he thought, he would make more horses like the lovely Panchita. And he would always remember her. But he would learn to make other things of the black pottery. He would make beautiful things that had never been made before. He would become one of the fine potters of the village.

ACO-6381   2/8/94

The types for this book are Sabon and Tiepolo, set by Typeworks, Vancouver, and Great Faces, Minneapolis. The book is manufactured by Edwards Brothers. Book design by Will Powers. Cover design by Will Powers and Cheryl Miller.

About the Author

The marriage between Joseph Geha's parents was arranged in Damascus, Syria, in the old Christian Quarter where his mother grew up. His father's hometown in nearby Zahleh, Lebanon, where Joseph was born was the traditional home of the Geha name, which dates back to premedieval times and was derived from a folklore character known throughout the Arab-speaking world as Djeha the Trickster.

In 1946 the family came to America. They made the trip in steerage on the first steamship out of Beirut Harbor after the war, went through Ellis Island, and settled in Toledo, Ohio, in an apartment above his father's grocery store.

Living in a largely Christian Lebanese-American community, Geha and his brother and sister spoke Arabic until they started school.

Most of Geha's work in poetry, prose, and plays is about families from the Middle East and the conflicts within an immigrant culture. His fiction has been anthologized in the *Pushcart Prize XV,* and is included in the Arab-American Collection of the Smithsonian Institution. In 1988 he was awarded a fellowship grant from the National Endowment for the Arts.

A single parent for many years to daughters Megan and Katie, Geha recently married novelist Fern Kupfer. They both teach at Iowa State University in Ames.

1 9 9 0

Through
and
Through

TOLEDO STORIES
BY JOSEPH GEHA

The Graywolf Short Fiction Series
GRAYWOLF PRESS · SAINT PAUL

Grateful acknowledgement is made to the editors of the following periodi-
cals, in whose pages many of these stories were originally published: *Epoch*
("Monkey Business"), *Amherst Review* ("Everything, Everything"), *Iowa
Review* ("Almost Thirty"), *Forum, #7* ("Something Else"), *Mississippi Val-
ley Review* ("News from Phoenix"), *Northwest Review* ("And What
Else?"), *Webster Review* ("Holy Toledo"), *Oxford Magazine* ("Through
and Through").

Publication of this book is made possible in part by grants from the National Endowment for the Arts, the Minnesota State Arts Board, and from
the Jerome Foundation. Graywolf Press is the recipient of a McKnight Foundation Award administered by the Minnesota State Arts Board, and has received generous donations from other foundations, corporations, and indi-
viduals. Graywolf Press is a member organization of United Arts, Saint Paul.

Published by Graywolf Press, 2402 University Avenue, Suite 203, Saint
Paul, Minnesota 55114. All rights reserved.

Library of Congress Cataloging-in-Publication Data
Geha, Joseph.
  Through and through : Toledo stories / by Joseph Geha.
     p.   cm. – (The Graywolf short fiction series)
  ISBN 1-55597-135-0 (paperback)
     1. Arab Americans – Ohio – Toledo – Fiction.   2. Toledo (Ohio) –
Fiction.   I. Title.   II. Series.
PS3557.E3544T48   1990   90-38118
813'.5 – dc20   CIP

A Paperback Original
First printing, 1990
9   8   7   6   5   4   3   2

In loving memory of my teacher,
Gregory Ziegelmaier
(1931–1969)

And in gratitude for the support
of the wonderful women in my life:
Megan, Katie, Gabi,
. . . and especially, Fern

Contents

Monkey Business

MAKE WAY! MAKE WAY! the marriage song begins. Its words, its slow, circular rhythms catch in the back of Zizi's mind as he waits for the streetcar — *the bride-groom walks with sureness* — and, absently, he begins to twist his wife's wedding ring around the knuckle of his little finger. *Make way.* Across the street the bums are waiting too, standing or leaning motionless beneath the green canvas awnings until the taverns open their doors for the evening. Zizi's eye follows the line of them, dirty feet in dirty shoes, as it stretches all the way to the Yankee Cafe on the corner.

And there, rounding the corner yet once more, comes the man in the sandwich sign, the bum they call Asfoori. He limps as he walks, one side of his face gripped by palsy into a blank and rigid smile. And he is filthy. Even from across the street Zizi can see where the sign (YAKOUB'S YANKEE CAFE AND GRILLE) is stained dark from bobbing up and down against his chin. Asfoori has circled the block a half-dozen times since Zizi began waiting for the streetcar. But this time a little boy is following him. It is Zizi's son, Jameel, limping and half-smiling in perfect imitation.

"You!" Zizi calls out. "Jimmy!"

The boy refuses to turn. He keeps his eyes fixed in a

flat, downward stare like the eyes of the man in the sandwich sign.

"Monkey!" Zizi shouts, but the two ignore him—the man because he is somewhat deaf, the boy because he is pretending to be—and they limp on past the line of bums, on to the opposite corner where they turn and disappear.

Zizi lets them go. What good would one more strapping do? The boy needs a mama; and now, across town this very minute, Zizi's bride-to-be is expecting him, waiting to receive the wedding ring of his dead wife.

Samira died in November, not quite five months ago, and Zizi realizes that his impatience to remarry is causing talk among the *ibn Arab,* whose families run most of the neighborhood's stores and taverns. Some are saying that Zizi's eagerness is nothing more than lust, and therefore improper. But not as improper, others are quick to add, as his choice of a new wife. Braheem Yakoub, Zizi's boss at the Yankee Cafe, has been against it from the first day he met the woman.

"Listen to me, Cousin," he told Zizi that day. "Every man pays for the love in bed—that's life—but the practical man doesn't pay too much."

And yet the love in bed has nothing to do with it. Even after all this time Zizi still does not miss it much. Frankly, it gave him nothing but trouble, especially at the start. It was the old country in the old days, and Zizi a son obedient to his father: the marriage had been arranged. On the wedding night Samira was expected to know nothing, like most brides in the old country. Zizi, for his part, simply thought that there was nothing much to know, presuming a kind of miraculous ease that is taken for granted in the stories boys overhear. But whatever it was was no miracle, and it certainly wasn't easy. Samira cried all that night and the next, and on the third night they didn't even try. Zizi dared not confess his failure; even so he quickly became the sub-

ject of village jokes. At last, a married cousin who was visiting from America—and who didn't think any of this was funny—took Zizi aside and explained everything, answered every question until both their faces were red: the how, the why, the when you do this or that. And he told him, too, to stop calling his penis by the baby name his mother had used and to call it instead his "Oldsmobile." That night Zizi showed his wife. And so much for the love in bed.

The streetcar is late. Zizi glances up at the sky, its single sheet of cloud lowering now with the promise of rain. It has rained every day this week, tonight will be no different. Even the air smells wet, and across the street the bums are huddling beneath the awnings like dirty children afraid of a bath. Zizi looks away from them, up to the top windows of the apartment building two streets beyond. A bedroom, a front room, a tiny kitchen, but when Samira was alive it had been a home. It had been a place where Zizi rediscovered what he'd had once before in his own father's house—the quiet, child-like confidence that here things would always be clean and, no matter what, he would be taken care of. It is this Zizi misses far more than the love in bed. Even now the memory of it remains, centered and epitomized in the one remembered image of a cup of coffee, Samira sitting at the kitchen table, drinking a cup of coffee.

And in his home she used to call him Nazir, his true name. What kind of a nickname is Zizi! A boyish diminutive, yet another reminder that he alone of the *ibn Arab* is not what they call "a practical man," the kind who earns his living in the employ of no other man; who has a home, a wife, children who obey his word; the kind of man who knows how to do things.

"... Watch me and I'll show you how. Watch. Watch," Braheem Yakoub keeps saying as he carves the meat from the bone. "Watch—" and his fingers dance so effortlessly as they mix spices with fat and filler, press-

3

ing it all into the funnel of the meat grinder. But Zizi cannot do it. Awed beneath the cold eye of a practical man, an impatient man nicknamed the Green Devil for his shrewdness in business, Zizi is always too slow or too clumsy, too easily confused. Usually, Braheem would have to take over the job himself ("Go on, move over"), sending Zizi off to do something simple, to bus dishes or wipe down the lunch counter.

He used to walk home after a day like that, and Samira would be there. She unlaced his shoes for him. She poured the coffee—always there was coffee—then she would sit with him at the kitchen table. Little Jameel was still in diapers when they came to America (in 1945, on the first ship to leave Beirut after the war), and the child used to sit like a puppy on the newspaper that covered the bare floor then, watching the two of them as they talked, his wet mouth working in silent imitation. Sometimes they laughed, and when they did, little Jameel would laugh too. . . .

And it is for Jameel, almost six years old now, that Zizi has decided to put Samira's ring on the finger of a strange woman. So that the boy will have a mama. *Make way.* He swats at the song as if it were a mosquito humming in his ear. The humming fades, then immediately sputters into the electric crackle of the approaching streetcar. As he steps out to wave it down, Zizi once again catches sight of Asfoori, with the half-smile and the sandwich sign, still limping his way around the block. And there, still following behind him, is Jameel.

"Jimmy!" Zizi shouts.

This time the boy looks, and Zizi gives him the warning gesture, thumb against the fingertips: Just you wait. Jameel promptly returns the gesture, then he, too, shouts something, but it is lost as the streetcar door hisses open.

("Monkey business," Braheem Yakoub calls it.

4

"Monkey see, monkey do – that's all it is. Don't worry, Cousin, he'll catch on.")

But sometimes the boy even acts like a monkey, jumping and scratching at his ribs, making monkey sounds that he calls "Ingleez" even though he can speak English better than any of them, without the slightest accent. No, it's more than simple childishness. Zizi had first noticed it just before Samira died, during those last weeks that she was in the hospital. Every morning and every afternoon he took an hour off work to visit her. Braheem Yakoub could have objected but he didn't. He understood. Even so, like a practical man, he hardly ever mentioned Samira. He talked business instead.

"Cousin, the day will come," he said one morning after Zizi and Jameel had returned from the hospital, "when the customers will order everything from machines, all of it wrapped up in waxed paper. They won't even see the waitress."

Zizi nodded. The doctors had told him not to expect miracles, and there were none. Samira was dying. He slipped the apron over his head and said nothing. Then after a minute Jameel spoke. Someday, he said, he would own a place like this. And when that day came he would sell everything in waxed paper – the burgers, the pie, even the chili. "God willing," Braheem Yakoub said, pleased. But the boy went on. He would marry an *Amerkani* woman, he said, and teach his children to speak only Ingleez, like the other monkeys. The pleasure immediately drained from Braheem's face, and he gave Zizi a quick glance.

Even at the funeral Jameel had acted strange, a boy of five standing tearless in front of his own mother's coffin, while Zizi himself had to be supported on either side by an uncle.

That was November. In February, after the commemoration ceremony, Zizi removed the black arm

5

band from his jacket, and that very night he spoke with Braheem Yakoub about finding another mama for the boy. Eventually, Braheem consulted Aunt Afifie; such things were, after all, really her business. The letters she wrote to the old country were shrewdly worded, never mentioning marriage, and yet their message was clear: a widower in America, a man of good family, has ended his mourning.

*

Cousins talked to cousins, and they agreed on just the girl, the daughter of a man in Aunt Afifie's old village overlooking the Syrian hills. In their letter of response they wrote that she was still young, not yet twenty-two. (So what if she was really closer to forty-two? In the mountains there were only church records, so who would know the difference?) The matter was quickly arranged, documents were signed on both sides of the ocean. The cousins, after payment to the father and the taking of their share, sent the old women to find the girl and inform her of the good news. They were told she would be somewhere in the nearby fields, sitting with a rifle, watching over her father's goats.

Uhdrah was staring hard at the brown hills when they came for her. Beyond those hills was Damascus where Holy Boulos was knocked from his horse and blinded by the light of Jesus. She did not hear them at first. She was talking with the saints, listening to their sad, premonitory voices when the old women came singing the marriage song.

> Make way! Make way!
> The bridegroom is tall,
> He walks with sureness. . . .

They told her, laughing and singing, that she was to be married, that she was to be sent to live in America.

No! the voices said. But she found herself smiling in

her surprise. She let go of the voices and laughed to hear
the news.

> Nazir is his name.
> His house is famous. . . .

No! But she said yes to her father and brothers,
blushing like a young girl as she said it.

*

After getting off the streetcar, Zizi still has a long walk
ahead of him to Aunt Afifie's house. There, Uhdrah has
been waiting since her arrival in America nearly a month
ago, awaiting the ring that should have been hers that
first week.

Zizi walks quickly along the darkening pavement,
but within several blocks of the house, he stops short.
There is a faint smell in the air, like incense. No, it
couldn't carry this far, his mind must be playing tricks.
He swats the thought away and continues walking.
Then, thinking anyway: it's not just the incense, there's
the rest of it too. Right at first he'd realized there was
something odd about the woman. It wasn't that she was
older than he expected her to be, nor that she was as
heavy in the hips and breasts as a mother of many children. On the contrary, he found all this somewhat at-
tractive. In a way it was even exciting – a grown woman,
a stranger, crossing an ocean for no other man but him.
What was odd, he discovered gradually that first week,
were her ways and the strange stories she told.

"She's new here," Braheem Yakoub shrugged when
Zizi mentioned the holy pictures that Uhdrah had hung
in Aunt Afifie's house, the rosaries and incense and little
figures of Jesus and Mary. "Besides, she comes from the
mountains. They're all that way in the mountains."

But Braheem was never around when Uhdrah told
her stories about how she had seen and actually spoken
with the Virgin, and about how, with the help of Saint

7

Maron, she had raised a dead goat to life. During those first days Braheem accused Zizi of making something out of nothing. "All right," Zizi said, "then see for yourself."

And Braheem did see. It was at the welcoming dinner in Uhdrah's honor. Salibah the butcher and Toufiq the mortician from Detroit—both of them cousins who would do anything for a joke—asked her about the stories. They kept their faces serious, as if truly interested, but the rest knew what was really going on. All except Uhdrah. She told them the stories, putting down her knife and fork so she could use her hands. She described the Virgin's voice which was like gentle water, and the little goat, so still, then trembling back to life. And she told a new story about how the voices of Holy Mikhail and Holy Raphael had directed her to a little pouch of Turkish gold buried in her father's field. The whole time Zizi's mouth hung open.

Then Toufiq, called Taffy up in Detroit, turned away and winked, and that was the signal. All around the table there were the snorts and chuckles of suppressed laughter. Even Jameel, whose face had been as serious as Taffy's, was snickering so that he had to spit back the milk he held in his mouth.

Uhdrah seemed oblivious to it all. She was looking at the light above the table, whispering to something up there as if in deep conversation. That made Zizi's spine tingle. Braheem Yakoub, too, was not laughing. He threw his fork into his plate then stared at Aunt Afifie. Aunt Afifie ducked her head a little and shrugged. . . .

Afterward, for nearly a month now, Braheem has been saying no, the practical man doesn't pay too much. Aunt Afifie says nothing at all. She doesn't have to because, finally, she is right. Each week Zizi pays Uhdrah a formal visit, each week Aunt Afifie gives him the fish eye, and her meaning is clear: a man like other men

doesn't waste time; a man like other men makes a home for his son.

And so now, like any other man, Zizi climbs the porch steps and presses the doorbell. The porch, the whole neighborhood, smells of incense. He presses the bell again.

"Awl ride! Awl ride!" It is Aunt Afifie's voice. "I yam coming!"

The old woman opens the door, and immediately her glance recedes into that look of bored disdain, the fish eye. Stepping aside, she takes Zizi's jacket and tells him to wait in the front room. Then, to show that there is nothing more to be said between them, she turns her back and goes into the kitchen.

Inside, the incense is stronger than he ever smelled it in church. Atop the mantel Uhdrah has placed a row of holy pictures rimmed in tooled leather frames from the old country: Saint Maron, patron of Lebanon; the Virgin of Fatima and of Lourdes; the Sacred Heart. And there is a new one that Zizi doesn't recognize. It is unframed, ragged on one edge as if taken from a book. A woman, near naked, but a saint—he can tell by the glow around her head—lies smiling on a pallet while gold coins fall toward her lap from a golden cloud.

Vigil candles flicker at each end of the mantel, like an altar. On the coffee table are tiny statuettes of the Holy Family, plaster things you win at parish fiestas. In the center, three cones of incense smolder on a silver dollar.

A door closes, and Uhdrah steps out of the hall bathroom, smoothing her hair with the palms of her hands. She who has crossed an ocean for his sake.

"Sit down, *Khawaja* Nazir." She uses the formal *Mister*. Zizi knows what this means: We are strangers until you give me the ring.

He does not sit down. "Uhdrah—" he begins, then

falters. Her eyes remain on him like the eyes of Jesus in the Sacred Heart picture, staring straight at you, waiting for the answer you have. Promising everything. He bows his head.

"Yes, *Khawaja?*"

His hand fumbles toward the ring in his pocket. Then, abruptly, he clasps his hands together and sits down.

"Do you have coffee?"

"Of course, *Khawaja*. If that is what you want."

After she is out of the room, Zizi sits perfectly still a while, listening to the cup-and-saucer sounds from the kitchen, the anxious, pigeonlike murmuring of the two women. It is April, past Easter, yet here next to an ash tray is the Christ Child in a manger. Thoughts come but he does not want to think them. He swats at them with his hand. "That is all," he says to drive them away. Then, taking Samira's ring out of his pocket, he places it on the table at the feet of the Christ Child.

Immediately Uhdrah sees it. She stops short in the hall, coffee sloshing onto the tray. She sets the tray down on the telephone table and hurries into the room, embracing Zizi before he can stand up. The ring is already on her finger. He did not see her put it on.

"My sweet one, Nazir," she is muttering in Familiar Arabic, "my eyes, my heart, Nazir!" She kisses him on both cheeks and on the forehead. "My baby, Nazir!" she says.

Samira, too, used to call him that. The coincidence thrills him, and he starts to smile. But, he reminds himself, this is for the boy's sake.

In the kitchen something clangs to the floor, bounces, and breaks. "Allah!" It is Aunt Afifie, a shout and a laugh at the same time. "Al-LAH!" She is thanking God.

Uhdrah sits back against the sofa cushions and, as if

a dam has burst, begins talking rapidly of the arrangements to be made, the wedding dress, the church, food
for the guests. Zizi continues to smile. He nods his head
now and then to show that he is a polite man, interested
in what is, after all, women's business. He can hear Aunt
Afifie singing in the kitchen. No, not singing, not words
anyway; more like a humming chuckle. After a time the
smile grows tight on his face.

Uhdrah has forgotten the coffee, beginning to cool
by now. As she talks—flowers, witnesses, invitations,
gifts—her fingers brush back and forth across Samira's
ring. It is on her right hand, according to custom. On the
wedding day she will wear it on her left.

Zizi does not want to smile anymore. He wonders if
it's started to rain yet. Then he thinks of the streetcar
schedule, but to look at his watch would be rude. Staring at the picture of the Sacred Heart, he makes a silent
request, and just as he does the telephone rings in the
hallway. By way of thanks, he lowers his eyes before the
picture.

"Awl ride!" Aunt Afifie shouts as the phone continues to ring. "I yam coming!"

Using this as an excuse to stand up and look at his
watch, Zizi explains that it is getting late, it might rain
any minute, and he dare not miss the last streetcar because if he does he'll have to call Braheem Yakoub—he
forces a knowing chuckle—and Braheem won't enjoy
having to drive all the way across town and back again.

Uhdrah glares at him, not even trying to mask her
displeasure. And why should she anymore?—the ring is
on her finger. Zizi is about to sit down again when Aunt
Afifie looks into the room.

"Nazir," she says, her face grim. "Braheem, he's
onna telephone. Asfoori's dead."

Instantly, Uhdrah makes the sign of the cross and
drops to her knees. Zizi cocks his head to show that he

does not understand. Asfoori is dead, too bad. Still, he was no relative, no reason to be making phone calls with the news. And Uhdrah, praying aloud on her knees, doesn't even know the man.

He takes the receiver, and Braheem tells him that Asfoori was walking the sandwich sign when, just a few minutes ago, he bent over to tie a shoelace, and simply died.

Zizi still doesn't understand. "After all, he's better off – right?"

"Right, Cousin. But that's not it. Your son was standing behind him when it happened. The boy saw it all."

Zizi stiffens and holds the receiver tight against his ear. "Is he scared bad?"

"No. But I don't think it's hit him yet. You better get here quick."

Uhdrah is still on her knees when he hangs up. "The man is only sleeping," she says, almost smiling. "Like Lazarus – "

"Quiet," Aunt Afifie says.

"When I was little, a baby goat they gave me died. My father was going to carve it up, but I took it and carried it into the fields. I ran until I heard a voice say, 'Your little goat is not dead but only sleeping.'" Uhdrah's face lights up with the memory. "It was Saint Maron's voice. He told me to put my hands on the goat, like this." She strokes the air back and forth with her hands.

"Stop that," Aunt Afifie says.

"And the little goat awoke from the dead." There is triumph in her voice. "Sometimes God gives the power."

"Hush, woman," Aunt Afifie says as she helps Zizi with his jacket.

"To those who truly believe, sometimes He gives the power."

*

Poor monkeys. That is what they are like with their big ears and the faces they make. Just like monkeys he has seen in the zoo and in jungle movies. The way they use their back legs to walk. And he is a monkey, too.

"... I tell you, Cousin, customers want to believe. That's why a practical man can fool them. They want to believe what their mama told them about everything. If their mamas put dog shit on a plate and said it was good, they'll eat it up and lick the spoon! The business-man says 'Look, I am just like your mama.'"

"How?" his father had asked. . . .

Braheem Yakoub's ears do not stick out, but if you look at them and only at them, they stick out. His nose is not large, but if you stare at it, his face is all nose.

"'How?' Watch the practical man. Do like he does. Don't ask how. Does the man slicing the liver know how he does it? Can he tell you? No. So don't ask, watch. Do like he does, Cousin, and then you'll know how."

"I still don't understand." His father still did not understand. . . .

They are just like monkeys if you look at them that way, making noises with their mouths, showing their teeth, using their hands to pick things up. Laughing sometimes and chattering, and sometimes looking sad. Scratching the sides of their faces when they are thinking, shaking their heads when they do not understand. Walking up and down the pavement, turning white when they are old. Making little noises when they are old. When they are dead, rolling over with their eyes shut. Lying very still, mouths open against pavement, against hospital pillows, poor monkeys. And he is a monkey, too.

*

The nickname Asfoori means "little bird." The *ibn Arab* called him that because he had spent several years in the state mental hospital, known to them as the *asfoori-yeh*

13

or "birdhouse." When he was released he was no good anymore for business, one side of his face frozen in that half-smile, all the English he had learned in America forgotten in the *asfoori-yeh*. He had no family, but he was *ibn Arab*, so Amos Salibah set up a cot next to the mops and buckets in the back room of his butcher shop. Asfoori did odd jobs, sweeping, walking the sandwich sign for Braheem Yakoub. They paid him in meals and lodging and spare change. It became his life, and now that he was dead, no one was terribly sad. He's better off, they say, and the arrangements that Taffy the mortician has made are for nothing more than a pauper's funeral.

Zizi, like the others, stands his turn taking coats and leading people to the casket. Asfoori was no relative, but they came nevertheless, out of simple charity, so that his death might not be completely ignored. "God give him rest," they say, and that is all. After the mops and buckets and sandwich sign, what else is there to say? "Bless His name," Zizi gives the standard response as he hands the raincoats and umbrellas to his son.

Jameel had been there, he saw how the old man turned the sandwich sign so he could bend down to tie a shoelace, how he didn't stop bending, instead made a quiet noise and rolled to the pavement with his mouth open. The boy saw, then he imitated even that. He, too, bent down, made a noise, and rolled sideways on his shoulder. (One of the bums, a war veteran, cried "Sniper!" and two or three others dropped to the ground.) When passersby ran to Jameel first, he abruptly opened his eyes and stood up and walked away.

Since that, Zizi has watched as Braheem instructed him to watch, but still there have been no tears and no bad dreams at night.

"Maybe," Zizi told Braheem, "it won't hit him until after the funeral."

"Maybe," Braheem said. "And maybe it already hit him."

Braheem never came near the casket ("He's dead, right? So where's the coffee?") and all evening he has been sitting in the adjoining room with several of the other older men. As at most funerals, Taffy would have cigars in there, coffee, and always a bottle to lace the coffee.

When Uhdrah arrives, followed briskly down the entrance way by Aunt Afifie, she begins weeping openly before she even reaches the room.

"*Ya Asfoori! Ya Asfoori!*" She launches into the funeral wail, but no one takes up the chant. Instead, the room buzzes as people turn to look and talk among themselves. Some are laughing outright: his real name was not Asfoori, and it sounds funny to wail: *O Little Bird!* Aunt Afifie grunts an embarrassed warning, and Uhdrah falls silent.

Taking their coats, Zizi leads the two women to the casket. Uhdrah kneels before it, but Aunt Afifie remains standing. The old woman makes a quick sign of the cross, glancing down only once as if to examine the quality of Taffy's work ("Awl ride," she whispers to Zizi), then she turns and walks quickly toward a chair far in the back.

Uhdrah has begun to pray, first only moving her lips, then making the breathy half-sounds of words. Whatever they are, they are not from the Prayers for the Dead. They are not even Arabic. She looks up after a while, listening although no one is talking now. The room has become quiet with watching her. For a full minute the only sounds are rain and the muffled voices of the men in the adjoining room.

"Uhdrah," Zizi whispers, but she ignores him. She separates her hands, like a priest giving benediction, then she places them on Asfoori's chest and begins to

stroke back and forth, muttering in that language no one in the room understands. Yet they know what she is doing. One way or another, they've all heard the story of the goat.

Her hands move gently along Asfoori's arm, the shoulder, the neck, the face (and just then Zizi thinks he sees the eyelids flutter – but no, he is staring too hard), the chest, down the belly, the waist.

"What'cha bet," someone says in a loud comic whisper, "she's gonna crank up his Oldsmobile too!"

And like a thunderclap everyone is laughing. Then Braheem is there, not laughing. And Aunt Afifie, shaking with anger as she grasps Uhdrah's hands from the corpse and spins her roughly around.

"Wait!" Braheem stares at Aunt Afifie. She understands. She takes the ring from Uhdrah's finger and gives it to him. Then, suddenly, the ring is in Zizi's hand. He does not know how it got there. So many people are talking at once. He puts the ring in his pocket. People chattering and laughing. Then Braheem motions, and Zizi follows him out of the noise.

It seems quiet in the car despite the wipers and the drum of rain on metal. All during the ride home Jameel, huddled alone in the back seat, says nothing. Nor does Braheem, who must have had a great deal of Taffy's "coffee"; he keeps the car at a crawl, weaving it slowly across the center line and then back again toward the curb.

Finally, stalling the engine in front of Zizi's apartment building, Braheem clears his throat to speak. "You're better off," he says. "But you shouldn't 'a let her do that to Asfoori."

"I saw his eyelids move," Zizi says firmly. Then, less firmly: "I thought I did. Besides, what if – "

"What if what? What if it worked? Say she did bring Asfoori back. Okay. But to what? So he can walk around the block some more?"

"God gives the power sometimes." That was how Uhdrah had said it. "To those who believe. And the goat, if it's possible for a goat, then maybe...," Zizi's voice trails off. He is not saying what he means to say. He means to say something for Jameel's sake, so young, sitting back there, listening.

"Goat? If Asfoori got up like the goat, what would people say? Tell me, Cousin. A miracle? How great is God? Not me. I'd say: Bad business." Braheem looks up toward the drumming roof. "Bad business!"

"The boy," Zizi whispers.

"Hah? Never mind, he catches on."

"Please." Then Zizi turns to his son. "Go on upstairs. I'll be up in a minute." Jameel nods but remains where he is.

"Hey —" Braheem says, looking up once more, "— why that old fart Asfoori and not this boy's mama who was young when she died?"

"Go on, Jimmy," Zizi says.

"Or why Asfoori and not Taffy's son who died in Detroit? What do you think, Cousin, would it heal Taffy's heart to see Asfoori jump outta that box?"

"Jimmy."

"Yes, Papa." Jameel opens the car door. He hesitates, then steps out into the rain and disappears beneath the wet shadow of the building. When the hall light winks on, Zizi turns again to Braheem. The old man's head is bobbing slightly, privately, as if in answer to a question nobody asked.

"Yep. But that's the trouble with miracles, Cousin. Wanna know what a practical man would say?" His voice drops, and Zizi has to lean in to hear him. "Why a goat — he would say — a goddam goat, and not me. You understand, Cousin? Me."

*

The rain is cold. Zizi stands a while in it, twisting Samira's ring around the knuckle of his little finger. His

clothes are getting soaked, but it feels good in a way, the rain dripping cold and clean from his hair. A practical man would laugh.

Going in, he tries to be quiet but the door closes loudly after him and his shoes make sucking noises on the stairs.

"Papa," Jameel stands at the bedroom door, laughing. "Lookit your shoes!"

Zizi looks. There is a puddle where he is standing; the top of one shoe has started to wrinkle, the other is curling up from the sole.

"Sit down, Papa." He takes Zizi's suit coat off. "I'll put this over the kitchen radiator." Zizi sits on the bed. He hears the sounds of the kitchen faucets.

Jameel returns with a clean towel. "Here." He hands Zizi the towel. "I put on some coffee." Then he kneels at his father's feet and begins loosening the shoelaces. Zizi lets him do it.

He lets him pull off the shoes, the stockings, lets him unbutton the wet shirt. The coffee has yet to boil, but already its smell fills the apartment. He swats at the thought of a mama. That is all.

The boy undoes the suspender straps. Then, grinning, he takes the ring from his father's finger and turns aside. When he turns back, the ring is on his thumb. It fits, and he keeps it there.

Zizi lets him. The boy will catch on—monkey see, monkey do. He will be a practical man someday. And that is all.

"Lift your legs." Jameel pulls the trousers off. "Now your arms."

Zizi obeys. Someday the boy will have his own business and sell all the food in waxed paper. And that is all. He will marry and teach his children to speak only English. But that is enough. That, and the smell of coffee in his house.

Everything, Everything

This has happened before to Barbara Saleeb. In times of strain her nerves will light upon some carefree tune and cling to it stubbornly. Like the time last winter, rushing her mother to the hospital. That time even the paramedics were sure it was the real thing — and all Barbara could think of as she knelt in the ambulance, squeezing Mama's hand, all that went around and around in her head, was the jingle to the Diet Pepsi commercial.

And here it's happening again. Ever since she came back from loading her dryer, Barbara has tried to ignore it, suppressing the urge to turn and stare down whoever that is standing behind her, impatiently rocking back and forth so that his cart full of wet wash is tapping against her shoulder, practically. Is it her fault she got the last available dryer? The whole time he's kept whistling — softly, full of breath and hesitation — but the same song over and over, with a melody so insistent that it's started repeating in her mind like a stuck record.

There's no telling what you're going to hear people singing or humming, or whistling down the back of your neck, ever since one of Toledo's top FM stations adopted an all-oldies format. She recognizes it, a Rosemary Clooney song from the fifties. Just the other day Uncle Junior was singing it along with the radio while he scraped down the butcher block. Barbara can even recall

snatches of the lyrics—something about apples, something about peaches and pomegranates.

She sighs pointedly and adjusts her magazine. But the man behind pays no heed, not here amid powdered bleach and fabric softener, diapers and boxer shorts— the insides-out of strangers. No, he keeps whistling away, rocking and whistling. Barbara can't even read. An invasion of privacy is what this is. She allows the magazine to slide off her lap, pauses, then slowly reaches down to pick it up.

He's not bad-looking, really. That much she can tell by a flickering once-over out of the corner of her eye. A longer, less furtive look confirms it: he's lean, clean-shaven, about her age, and the kind of American blond whose arms look hairless, smooth, almost shiny.

But why would he stand there and let her look at him this way, directly up and over her shoulder, without acknowledging her glance? Probably because he's looked already. There isn't a sign of hair in the open vee of his shirt collar. Clean. Barbara lowers her glance. Even his fingernails are clean. He's not wearing a wedding ring.

Abruptly, the whistling stops, the man shifts his stance, and Barbara turns, almost jerks, back to the magazine on her lap. She remains that way, frozen, and then crosses her legs, posing almost, as if in accordance with some unspoken protocol among strangers: I looked, and now it's your turn. She is glad she changed into shorts after work; pushing the season a bit, this far into autumn, but her legs always have been her best feature, trim with small ankles. Year-round swimming at the Y keeps them in tone. Feeling the heat of his glance, Barbara focuses on one knee, on a few hairs that she missed shaving the night before, and then on a stray thought of her mother wandering the wide causeways of the mall, right this very moment probably, in that top-

heavy duck walk of hers, arms pressed to her sides with the purse bounce-bumping to the gait, until the whistling resumes.

*

"Something he's in there, Beebee?"

Even now, remembering, Barbara must take a deep, calming breath. The whole time in the car Mama'd kept at it when all Barbara wanted was to be left alone.

"What more do you want?" Barbara was being a good girl, she was going out of her way, in fact, miles past the laundromat, to drop her mother off at the mall. So Mama wouldn't be bored tonight. What more did she want of her, what more could she find to complain about? "You want it all, Mama? Everything?"

"I mean just about him." Mama indicated the glove compartment with her hand but she didn't touch it.

They'd been arguing on and off ever since Barbara got back from work, but later, in the car, her mother's voice had turned accommodating, polite. And somewhere along the line she'd switched to English. "Something you don' wan' me to see him?" She shuffled her feet. She had on her black shoes. "Maybe he's a secret?" Ordinary black shoes, plain, practical. Nun's shoes, Uncle Junior called them, and even Mama would smile.

"There's nothing in there, Mama."

"Nat'ing?" A question, but so disbelieving that it promised yet another argument. And over what this time? A magazine, Barbara's *Opera News,* which she'd perched behind the sun visor. As they were slowing for a stoplight it had dropped lightly, almost in slow motion onto Barbara's lap. And the argument? The terrible dark reason for this promise of an ugly scene? Barbara had wanted to replace the magazine behind the sun visor, while Mama had expected her to put it in the glove compartment.

"Nothing, Mama."

"Nat'ing." Now not a question. Arms folded over her purse in a hunched posture that says "Lies, too, I bear as Christ bore the cross."

"Except, you know, glove compartment stuff." Old women from the old country, they keep themselves helpless on purpose. They never learn to drive a car, not even to sign their own names in English. No, they'd rather sit there and wait for you to undo your seat belt and get out and go all the way around the car to open the door for them, give them an arm to brace against the ordeal of lifting their own weight from a car seat. And what is Mama, ten pounds overweight? No more than that. And how old, fifty-one? fifty-two? If there's such a thing as hysterical pregnancy, Barbara wonders, might there also be such a thing as hysterical old age?

"Whad stuff, Beebee?"

"I don't know. Just stuff."

"Oh."

And if so, if believing makes aging so, is such a quality inheritable, like family madness? An especially disturbing thought because otherwise the resemblance between them is as undeniable as it is, to Barbara's eyes, unfortunate: both of them dark-haired, hairy—every Saturday their upper lips tweezed identically red and sore; both of them short, tending to heaviness, and more than well-endowed, much much more—to Barbara's eyes both of them preposterously, humiliatingly busty. Two of a kind, Papa used to say.

Without another word Mama took the *Opera News* from behind the sun visor and reached for the glove compartment knob.

"Do *not* open it." Barbara clipped her words, investing them with the authority of command: she was the driver, this was her car, every switch and dial and knob of it was hers. "I want it where I had it. All right?"

Her mother didn't answer, so Barbara made a hasty, clutching gesture with one hand. And still nothing, only

Mama's large bosom rising with stubbornness. Barbara almost snapped her fingers. At the office her boss did that to her sometimes when she was slow to pick up on what he wanted. Finally, in one deliberate motion, Barbara snatched the magazine away and replaced it behind the sun visor.

"Awl ride, Beebee. Yokay." Jesus forgiving his executioners.

Barbara breathed out against the snugness of her blouse and said "Mama...," but didn't know what else to say. She hadn't intended to be mean.

"You show, Beebee, he gonna start soon?"

"I don't know, Mama. Maybe." On baseball weekends WJR usually taped the Metropolitan Opera for delayed broadcast later in the week. Mama's voice exaggerated concern.

"You don' wanna hear him, you show?"

"What if I don't? Huh?"

"Nat'ing, Beebee, nat'ing."

Nothing, nothing. Of course nothing. Which was what all this motherly attention was supposed to cover over, the fact that Barbara's passion for music has always been nothing to her mother. Papa might have understood, but he died before she'd seen her first opera. And as for the rest of them, the aunts and uncles and cousins, it's less than nothing, more like a favorite joke. "Nutsy," Uncle Junior calls it. Over the years Barbara's response to their teasing has been silence and the strength of her own stubbornness. After all, is there any reply to "Nutsy"? Is there any reasoning with a gray-haired uncle who wears a black toupee?

And as for tonight's broadcast, even though it is *Don Giovanni*, even though Mozart is one of her favorites, right then, driving out of her way to the mall, Barbara wanted only a little quiet, like the hush the tires were making on the wet pavement—shh, shh.

"Shh, Beebee? Howse come you say that?"

"My God, I'm just breathing."

"Howse come you breat'ing shh?"

"I don't know, can't I breathe?"

*

Immediately, as soon as her dryer finishes its cycle, as soon as Barbara begins wheeling her empty wash cart down the long aisle toward it, the man does exactly what she expected him to do: he lock steps directly after her with his own cart.

She pushes on, and the whistling follows close behind, so very close in fact that she glances over her shoulder once, quickly – only to discover that, of course, it's just her imagination; he's keeping his distance. And yet, as she quickens her pace, the whistling quickens, too, or so it seems now in her imagination, following directly behind her up to the dryer door (something about giving away peaches, pomegranates, too), in her imagination hovering over her shoulder as she scoops her things – some of them private things – in hot, crackling armfuls from dryer to wash cart. The whistling gains on her, so fast-clipped now and insistent (giving away candy, giving away something, then something else), as if prodding her on. And then he really is that close, one hand on the dryer door. Quickly, she stuffs the last of her underthings beneath a bath towel and hurries the cart to the privacy of a corner table.

Barbara glances at the clock above the candy machines. If she hurries she might not miss the beginning of the broadcast, the opera's slow *andante*. But a car was no place to listen to it, especially with her mother sitting next to her, one minute pouting like a child, the next making clumsy amends. No, best of all was alone.

Alone on the daybed of her own apartment, shoes kicked off, the headphones turned up loud; only then could Barbara close her eyes and really allow the music to take over. Soon, always, she would find herself adrift in a reverie of favorite thoughts: living the rest of her life

within walking distance of the Met, being good friends with Beverly Sills and Leontyne Price; being slim and, even more important, small-busted; seated in the guest loge, basking in the spilled glow of the overhead gels, listening to an aria sung that night just for her, one long, sad, controlled wail of notes fading to a silence that is brief, absolute, until shattered by a sustained explosion of applause.

None of it possible, of course, she's always known that. And yet, if only small-busted, if only that; if not pleasure, then at least absence of the one long pain of her growing up. In elementary school she'd been no more prepared for the initial envy of the other girls than for their pity afterwards in junior high as she continued to grow and as, finally, their cool dismissing shrugs became even more painful than the outright snickers of the boys. Oh, the boys, those straight-faced boys who asked her out for dates they never intended to keep, who purposefully squeezed past her in the crowded hallways ("Pardon me." "Pardon me again." "Gee, pardon me *again!*"), who cast long, indecent stares at her, and one who even reached his pencil across the aisle in senior study hall to poke at her and poke at her until finally she stood up, clumsy with books and note pads, and moved to another seat, reluctant, ungainly, feeling like a prodded cow.

But in the winter of that same senior year, everything began to change. For Christmas Uncle Junior presented Barbara and her mother with opera tickets he'd won in a Rotary Club raffle. It was the first time Barbara had ever been to an opera, and she took Christmas mints along in her purse to ease the inevitable boredom. The opera was Donizetti's *Lucia di Lammermoor,* and by the time the famous mad scene had begun she'd forgotten completely about the mints. It came upon her simply, suddenly, with the rising of the voices, the vibrations that swelled out of the orchestra so that she found herself trembling.

It occurred to her that she was hearing the music with her entire body, that every quaver and rumble seemed to be seeking entrance not only to her ears but to every part of her, touching everything. Then a single voice rose above the rest. The sweetness pierced her. Barbara had never thought such sweetness possible, so painful in its urgency. At first she felt herself retreat until, resolve melting, glistening, she surrendered to it, the trembling giving over to tears. They poured out, and wouldn't stop all the scene long. Nor did she want them to stop. Afterward she leaped up, startling Mama out of a doze, and shouted as she heard the others around her shouting *Brava! Brava Diva!*

Things began to change after that night. Barbara decided on her own apartment; she enrolled in evening accounting classes and early morning aerobic swimming. For a while she even considered risking an operation that would reduce her bust size. But in this her resolve had faltered: she could just imagine her mother's reaction, the gasp and heave of Mama's own voluminous bosom as she listened, building probably to that familiar hands-in-the-air yell of hers—"Yii-i-i!"—as if somebody'd spilled coffee in her lap; then no doubt rushing back to tell Uncle Junior, slapping her hands against the butcher block and jabbering angrily in Arabic, while Junior, bent over a carcass of lamb, his toupee hanging on a nail with the saws and cleavers, would have to put down the curved knife and try to quiet her—"Shh, shh"—himself shocked by it all.

But it never happened that way. Mama had remained calm while Barbara told her about it. "My Heart, why look for trouble?" she said in Arabic, and it was all she said. Then her eyes narrowed and her mouth turned tight-lipped, defiant, as if calling a bluff. And it was only then that Barbara realized that it actually was a bluff, that she'd never really intended to have the operation. In fact, from the moment that the idea had begun

to present itself as a genuine possibility, there had occurred simultaneously in her mind's eye a sad, defeating comparison between cosmetic surgery and...well, Uncle Junior's toupee. What discouraged her even more was the irrevocability of it, with absolutely no assurance as to how she would look afterward. At least Uncle Junior could remove his hairpiece, hang it on a nail.

And so the advice that Barbara gave herself was, finally, her mother's advice: Why look for trouble?

*

Barbara can't help watching the man. She cranes out into the aisle – her hands absently refolding a dishcloth – for a clearer look. And what a sight he is, struggling away at a still-damp sheet. He really doesn't know what he's doing; his wash could hardly be dry after only one cycle. Those shirts hanging damp on their hangers will probably dry against the car seat with all their wrinkles pressed into them. Barbara smiles wryly to herself, almost fondly. Then instantly the smile vanishes and she feels her heart drop. He has pulled a nightgown from the heap. It is a woman's summer nightgown, filmy, white with pale blue piping down the front.

He holds it high, and Barbara imagines how tall his wife must be to wear it, and slim. His wife would be suntanned probably, against all that white. Yes, suntanned, even though summer is ended; just the same, suntanned, and white teeth laughing.

Then he is folding a flower-patterned sheet, looping it over one arm to keep it from dragging on the floor. Then a beige slip, and Barbara can see how puzzled he is (the soft whistle dropping to a hesitant trickle – rice, spice, something, everything nice) as he glances from the hanger in his one hand to the slip in his other. Hang a slip? He doesn't know what he's doing. He solves the problem by crisscrossing the thin straps around the neck of the hanger. He holds it up high. She must be taller than her husband, Barbara thinks, slim in white or beige

against flowered sheets. Next he picks up a bra. It is candy pink, and sheer—no wires or reinforced stitching. He folds something else pink—a camisole?—first one way then another, and finally tucks it uncertainly away among the towels and his own cottons. He drapes a nurse's uniform onto a hanger. He folds a lacy half-slip, folds its matching bra.

Barbara isn't surprised at what happens next. She can't have known that just then he would hold up another brassiere, but thinking back on it later it will seem that she knew, the way a dreamer sometimes knows what is coming next: curious, yet not at all surprised to see familiar things shift inevitably into nightmare, not at all surprised to see that this brassiere is different from the others—plain, practical white cotton, triple hooked at the back, its huge cups braced stiff with elastic and underwire. Then, dreamlike, Barbara finds that she is moving her hand from side to side in front of her, erasing a blackboard. In grade school and junior high some of the girls used to do that when they misspoke themselves during recitation. She lowers her hand.

He's noticed nothing. In his impatience, he has simply folded the brassiere and placed it atop the pile. And now he is folding away a few remaining hand towels, stuffing them into the sides of his laundry basket.

Barbara edges furtively up to the door, begins to ease it open, but then steps back. The door hisses shut in front of her.

He is finished. Draping the hanged clothes over one arm, he lifts the basket and makes for the door. Barbara moves aside to let him pass. Even so he nearly brushes against her, turning to push open the door with his back. Her brassiere, unfolding against its heavy stitching, sits perched atop his laundry like a baby's bonnet. She watches it pass by, little rust stains at the hooks, the big cups jouncing happily. Then it is out the door. A car

starts, headlights beam then turn away. And it is gone. As simply and as suddenly as that.

*

Would he bring it back? Or would the two of them simply have their laugh over it ("Good God, where'd *this* come from?") and keep it, put it away somewhere? Yes, somewhere with the odds and ends, in the back of a drawer, maybe, where it would remain forever along with his unmatched socks.

Next to her, Mama sighs a prolonged geriatric sigh.

For blocks now her mother's been preparing to get out. Barbara doesn't have to look, she knows from the familiar little rustles of motion that now the coat is being buttoned, now the purse strap pulled tight to the wrist, one hand already on the door latch, black shoes poised ducklike for the stepping down. And Barbara doesn't want to look. The thought of having to wait for Mama to get out, of having to sit there and watch that slow duck walk until the porch light finally snaps off and she can drive on to her own apartment – is enough to dispel a fragile lightness she feels summoning her just now: imagine being forgotten, tucked privately away in a drawer in their house forever; outside it would be raining, and from downstairs, faintly, would come the ordinary sounds of a house – TV, the dishwasher, people talking; mornings, so cozy with rain outside, his wife asleep beneath the flowered sheets; him whistling as he shaves, apples and spice and something, something nice. . . .

Ahead now is the old house, its porch light a yellow glow approaching out of the darkness of the maple trees. Barbara downshifts, making a slow wide arc into the driveway, and her mother has the door open almost before the car comes to a full stop. But then Mama pauses, the door swung wide and the air rushing in cold and damp, and after a moment she turns and settles

back again in her seat. She says nothing, she simply stares Barbara full in the face as if expecting—what? Good night?

"Good night."

Mama doesn't respond. Her face, shadowed from above by the dome light, is defiant, inviting trouble, and so is the accompanying motion of her hand, just asking for trouble, thumb and forefinger reaching precisely for the glove compartment knob.

Barbara's feet slip trembling off the pedals. "Mama!" The engine shudders, then cuts out completely.

In the silence there is a sound so low, so quiet, at once private yet rising out of its privacy, that she thinks it might be the sound of her own voice. But no, she turns, sees the quiver of Mama's parted lips, the sound swelling out of them to a low secret wail like singing except uncontrolled, untrained. Barbara cannot help remarking that it must have begun somewhere near the baritone range—an odd sound to come out of a woman—before she claps both hands over her ears.

"Shh," she says. "Shh," even after the sound bends, fades, as if returning once more into the silence of its privacy, "shh," over and over, only gently now, lingeringly, "shh," as if to herself, just as once she herself had wanted hushed the frightened sounds of her own long childhood, the noise of study period and gym class and cafeteria.

She keeps both hands over her ears even as, slowly, she looks up again, up the familiar curves of that body, and sees that Mama's bosom, like Barbara's own, is surging up and down for breath. Poor thing, how could she have been so mean to her? Up and down and up together, the unison is almost perfect. Two of a kind.

Poor things, both of them. Heads hunched meekly, identically, hands gripped in their laps, the fingers working, working, chests heaving for air. Like swimmers.

How strong Mama is; meek, yes, and helpless, and yet strong. Then, simply, suddenly, it occurs to Barbara that they might be drowning, the two of them, that they might die from this. Where do swimmers find such strength in their last moments, swimmers clinging as they go down?

Quickly, Barbara reaches past her mother and opens the glove compartment door, with both hands scoops out several matchbooks, a package of breath mints, a road map. These she places on her mother's lap. She takes out a sample bottle of cologne, a pencil, a barrette, a street guide of Toledo, a packet of postage stamps. All into her mother's lap, everything, ticket stubs, a penlight, a tin of aspirins, some pennies, some paper clips, everything, until, like a close call, it is over.

Dazed, chest heaving for breath, she sits back. In the stillness of the neighborhood even the maple leaves hang motionless against the street lamp. Next to her Mama is taking air in quick little gasps that cause the clutter on her lap to slide gradually down her dress and drop piece by piece onto the floor. Barbara fixes her eyes on Mama's shoe, a matchbook on the toe of the shoe, and waits for Mama's move. It doesn't come. Nor does that song, now that she thinks of it, so lighthearted and funny and, no, she can't recall a word of it anymore. The next move is her own, then, and each one after that.

Almost Thirty

My father, Rasheed Yakoub, never got used to the snow and the long winters of this country. In the middle of a January or February he would walk home from work at the restaurant and grumble and stamp the snow from his shoes on the back porch. It would be dark outside, though only supper time. My mother always had his supper waiting, rolled grape leaves, or lamb meat ground with cracked wheat, or raw liver and onions. And in the winter when it snowed, he always told her to keep the food warm while he rested a little. Sitting next to the radio, he would grumble and devote long Arabic curses to the snow of this country, how it never stopped coming, how it stayed when it came, until my mother would tell him to hold his peace, or at least curse in English for the children's sake. My two sisters pulled the wet shoes from his feet, and I scratched his head with my fingernails. My father had a large black moustache, but he was an old man and the hair on his head was white all the years I knew him.

On a Sunday in late April, when I was a little boy, wet snow began to fall as my mother got us ready for church. My father, who did not go to church, was still in bed when the rest of us sat down to breakfast. His room was next to the kitchen, and we could hear him get out of bed and pull up the window shade. My sisters looked

across the table at me, their dark eyes laughing. We were waiting for the string of curses to begin, for it was spring now and not the time for snow. There was silence, only the sound of spoons and forks. My father came into the kitchen, unshaven and looking glum. Lila, the youngest, began to giggle and I bit my lip for a long time. But my father said nothing about the snow.

By the time church was over the snow had stopped and the sun came out warm and melting. Leaving dinner to the females, my father and I walked through the slush to Walbridge Park. We looked at the yellow flowers, bowed almost double and dripping under the snow. I was holding his hand. "Do not feel bad, hold your peace," he said in Arabic, although I did not feel bad. "The time has come for spring." Then he spoke in English, something like "Goddamn it."

Among the family, among my countless aunts and uncles and cousins, it is still said that Rasheed Yakoub loved a good joke more than anything, if it was told well. And he would listen to it again and again, and laugh each time, if it was told well. He had been a schoolteacher in the old country, but in America he ran a small restaurant with his brother, Uncle Najeeb. For many years Uncle Najeeb (while he was alive) and his wife and their son, George, lived upstairs from us in a duplex apartment. During these years when our two families shared the same roof, George and I grew up like brothers.

What I have to tell has to do with my father Rasheed, who hated snow and who loved, above all things, a good joke, if it was told well. And more, this is about my cousin George who grew up several years be-hind me, like a little brother; George who, as he stum-bled toward his mid-twenties (and I myself neared, reached, and miraculously passed thirty), suffered from bad dreams and worried about his health, counting the beats of his heart and the breaths he took by the minute;

who could not dance, neither the ballroom waltz nor the stamping, snake-dancing *debkee* of our own mother country, Lebanon. Especially, this is about dancing and a family picnic in 1969 when George Yakoub threw down an egg salad sandwich and, letting his heart and lungs and feet do what they would, danced.

My father died of cancer in January of 1964, and I remember him best as he was the last time I told him the story of the rabbi and the priest — white-faced against the hospital's white sheets, his voice loud with laughing, and the nurses rushing in to find out what was the matter. That happened when I was almost thirty.

*

Alone on a Friday night that same winter, I was only a little nearer to thirty, and thinking about that fact, and about my father's death, and other facts. The room I rented, with its single bed, its armchair, and Halicrafter television, was one flight up from my Uncle Habeeb's supermarket on Monroe Street. When I returned from the navy in 1959, I had decided to begin college as a freshman. Uncle Habeeb gave me a part-time job in his new store, which was half a mile uptown from the small place, torn down now, where he'd got his start. He rented me the room some time after I began working there, a time when, after much fighting, much cursing from my father and tears from my mother, I saw that I had changed and could not live at home anymore.

In those days after my father's funeral, although I still attended classes, I could not read or study. I was doing nothing. It was Friday night and I had been drinking a little and watching the late movie. I had been thinking about some things I knew were facts and I was smoking too many cigarettes. The movie ran on, a horror story, I think, from the early fifties, a bad one, so I called my cousin George at his home. He was living with his mother then, in 1964, when he was nineteen and I was twenty-six. His father, Uncle Najeeb, had died before

34

George finished grade school. Like me, George was the son of old parents.

Aunt Anissa answered the phone, George's mother. My call had awakened her, and her voice was far away with sleep. I told her I was sorry. "It is nothing, Haleem," she said in Arabic, "I was not sleeping." Aunt Anissa knew me, so she knew I must have been drinking to call at such an hour. "It is nothing," she said again. George was not home; he had gone, she said, to a play at the university. Then she asked me what time it was. I told her it was near midnight, and she said George should be at the restaurant by now, helping to close up. I thanked her. "Try to go back to sleep," I told her, and she laughed because she hadn't fooled me.

I sat by the phone a while, looking out the window on Monroe Street. Behind me the movie ran on to its end; I heard the sermonette, then the national anthem. Outside, traffic was thinning and Monroe Street was becoming quiet. Soon the street would be so quiet you could hear footsteps. I was almost out of cigarettes, so I turned off the television and walked down the back stairs to my car.

The restaurant still had a fairly good crowd, the weekend pie-and-coffee people who came in after the movies to read newspapers and stay a long time. George was clearing tables, serving coffee. He did not see me at first. I bought cigarettes from the machine and sat in a booth near the kitchen. George was very busy, hurrying up and down the two aisles of the restaurant, limping because he was tired. He had not bothered to change his white shirt from the play, or to take his tie off even. He had tucked a towel in his belt as an apron. You could not see the belt because of his stomach. His cheeks looked very full and the glasses slid down his face from the hurrying and the sweat. *Muskeen*, I thought. We called George this sometimes, but never to his face. It means poor fellow, and though we said it only in the

kindest way, we had to say it since he was so clumsy, fat in his belly and rear, since he did not know how to comb his curly hair, and even the barber could do nothing but cut it off again and again. He was *muskeen*, too, because he was the only one of our family to ever need glasses, and he limped when he was tired. ("Only a *div'da'a*, a frog, would get hurt in grade school football," I told him when he was twelve, and then he dislocated his hip in the first scrimmage game.) *Muskeen*, I thought. George saw me, but he did not look too happy.

"Haleem," he said, and poured me coffee. "Stay a little—we'll stop serving in a minute."

I waited, and after a little George poured himself some coffee and sat down with me. His face was very serious, making it look even chubbier. "I did it again," he said. He clicked his tongue, tch, and looked down into the coffee cup.

"Did what, Jorgi?"

"Tch," he said again. I opened the new package of cigarettes and took one out.

Then he told me what he did. He told me the way a boy tells a priest his sins. After the play that night, which was a musical show, the performers had gone into the audience and asked the people to come up on stage and dance with them. A very pretty girl had asked George.

"She was very pretty," he said, "and she even touched my shoulder when she asked me." He paused, and I lit the cigarette. This was an old story with George.

"You said no?"

"Am I crazy, Haleem?" He was talking in Arabic now. "I looked down at my shoes and I told her no thank you."

He said tch...tch again and traced the rim of the coffee cup with his finger. I tried to make a joke.

"I'll bet Cary Grant would've got up and danced," I said to him.

"I wanted to, so why didn't I? Am I crazy, Haleem?"

"I'll bet President Johnson would've got up and danced."

He said tch...tch.

"I'll bet you Jiddo Braheem would've got up and danced."

That made him laugh, for Jiddo Braheem was a very old man and the way he limped and shook when he danced at family picnics made us laugh sometimes, even though he was the grandfather of all of us and we loved him.

George laughed and he said, "Yes, Jiddo Braheem would've got up and danced — but did I get up and dance?"

"I'll bet Uncle Yousef would've got up and danced."

"Yes," George laughed, "Uncle Yousef would've got up and danced — but did I get up and dance?"

"I'll bet Danny the dishwasher would've got up and danced," I said.

This happened in March of 1964, two months after my father died, when George was nineteen and I was twenty-six.

*

Jiddo Braheem Yakoub, called the Green Devil, was the first of our family to come to America. This was in the twenties when there was money, prohibition, and no jobs. Braheem was well past middle age then, but strong. He found work as a peddler and later drove a produce truck for a Greek named Sophanakoluros. By the autumn of 1929 Braheem had saved enough to send for his wife and children and his cousin Afifie who had been to school and could speak English. They unpacked their things, Aunt Afifie told us many times, and every channel on the radio was talking about the stock market. "On the radio," she told us, "the crazy Americans were jumping out the windows," and she laughed at this. "Goddamn, goddamn," she said, and she laughed.

The produce business failed, so Braheem and the Greek Sophanakoluros began driving their truck for a local bootlegging ring that was part of a larger, more serious operation out of Detroit. During this time Braheem made "a heap a' greenbacks" and got out of the business before the "dicks" ever caught on. Americans began calling him the Green Devil. He laughed at this name. "You betcha," he told them, "Goddamn, you betcha," and he crossed himself with three fingers lest his luck should change.

Braheem opened the Yankee Grille with his money, and later a restaurant that served American and Cantonese food because a Chinese cook was all Jiddo Braheem could find. (By 1967, the year he died, the business had expanded into a chain of three restaurants throughout the city, two Chinese and one steaks-and-chops, each operated by a different member of the family.) His cousin Elias arrived from the old country, Uncle E, whose seriousness the old ones say I inherited, and Braheem started him in a grocery on Monroe Street. Uncle E's wife died in 1938, and he did not live long after her. His nephew Habeeb took over the store. In later years Habeeb would be the first of our family to marry an American, and Aunt Afifie would refuse to go to the wedding, saying that Habeeb had become crazy like the Americans.

When the United States entered the Second World War, Braheem sent two of his sons to the army, and in 1946 these two returned unharmed, with no stories to tell and no medals to speak of, but unharmed, and ready to go to work.

The Mediterranean shipping lanes opened with the war's end, and my family arrived, and George's family. (The whole journey I was sick with typhus. I can remember clearly only one incident—my father holding me up to a porthole to see the dolphins jump. Because of the typhus our ship was delayed at Ellis Island for two

weeks.) Others came then too, old Uncle Yousef who had studied for the priesthood and quit, and never married; the family musician Uncle Abd'Allah (like so many of the others, not really my uncle but a cousin of one sort or another), who was Dominic and Aboodi's father; Uncle Nazir and his son Jimmy; Uncle Taffy; Aunt Yemnah, who married a Syrian from Damascus and moved to Cleveland with him. More came, some not related at all, but just the same, cousins and uncles and aunts.

Uncle E and his wife died first. Then Jiddo Braheem's wife died of her old age. Aunt Yemnah died in Cleveland some years after that. The Greek Sophanakoluros died in a rest home in Florida without my ever meeting him. George's parents, Aunt Anissa and Uncle Najeeb, had a baby boy when it was past their time, and the child died without ever seeing light and nearly took his mother with him. Uncle Najeeb died when George was still in grade school. Habeeb's first son was killed in the early days of Vietnam. Then in 1964, when I was almost thirty, my father died.

*

Throughout the funeral, throughout the mourning and the time of quiet that followed my father's death, George stayed by me and worried over me like a little brother. He brought me cigarettes and coffee, sat up with me in my room till all hours when neither of us had anything to say. I learned later that, *muskeen*, he even carried a capsule of smelling salts in his pocket. He sat next to me at the funeral breakfast, and when he left the table to get more cigarettes for me, Aunt Afifie blessed him behind his back. "*Muskeen*," she said to my mother, "Jorgi and Haleem, they are like brothers." It was the truth, but my mother only nodded over her coffee. Aunt Afifie had said this many times. She said it when George was little and I tried to teach him football, and again she said it when I was out of the navy and

39

George sat with me at the kitchen table, showing me how to fill out the forms for school. "Haleem and Jorgi, they are like brothers." She said this once at a family picnic in Walbridge Park, years ago, when George was not yet out of grade school and his father was dead only a little while. It was springtime. Uncle Abd'Allah began picking and strumming the lute while his sons, Dominic and Aboodi, beat time to the music on little Arab drums. They were making music for the *debkee,* which begins slow and becomes frantic and stamping. Jiddo Braheem was leading the dance. Slowly, he locked arms with Uncle Yousef, and the snake began there. With his free right hand, slowly at first, Braheem waved and spun the great red handkerchief he always carried. I wanted to join the dance before things got dizzy. "Jorgi!" I called to my cousin because I wanted him to join the dance, too. On purpose he did not notice me. He stood by Aunt Afifie at a picnic table where the old ones were puffing on water pipes and playing cards. "Jorgi!" I called him again. He did not look up. Aunt Afifie was playing solitaire and, on purpose, George was watching the hand she had laid out for herself. So I pulled him by the arm. My father came up from behind and gave me a slap. "Let your cousin be," he said. George ran back to Aunt Afifie and stood at her shoulder. She put down her cards. She looked up at my father and began to say something very softly. Her throat needed clearing.

"What's that?" my father asked before she had finished. He was watching the dance.

Aunt Afifie cleared her throat. I cleared my own throat to hear her. "Haleem and Jorgi, they are like brothers," she said.

My father did not look at her. He had one end of the black moustache in his mouth and he was watching the *debkee.* "I know, I know," he said to her in Arabic. Then he left us and broke into the *debkee* next to my mother and joined the dance.

"Haleem is like your brother," she said to George. She seemed to think of something. "Goddamn, goddamn," she laughed and she cleared her throat. "Not like the crazy Americans."

George did not answer Aunt Afifie, and I joined the dance where my father opened it up to let me in.

*

George did not dance at the picnic, as he did not dance with the actress who touched his shoulder more than ten years later. So, "Jiddo Braheem would have got up and danced," I said to him that night in the restaurant, and we laughed.

We got drunk that night. George finished up, and we drove to a tavern near the university. It was closing time, but the bartender let us in. I knew him from school. His name was Johnny O'Dwyer, and I used to joke with him about being half Irish, half French, half English, and half German — like every American I ever met. Johnny drank with us while the waitress wiped tabletops and carried empty mugs to the three sinks behind the bar. We drank together, and soon we were talking about crazy things.

"Everybody dreams in black and white," I said, when our talk had got around to dreams. "You only remember them in color when you wake up." I heard these things in a class at school.

"Then how do you figure this?" George said to me. "Last month I had this dream. You were driving my Chevy, and I was sitting next to you. We stopped for a red light. It was red. I can still see the color."

I did not know how to figure that, so I shrugged. Johnny did not look too happy with our talk. He was sliding a quarter from hand to hand on the bar.

"Just as you stopped for the light," George said, "the Chevy stalled. And all of a sudden your father was in the back seat. He sort of leaned up between us and he said 'It died on you.' He said it in Arabic."

George waited for me to say something, but I was

drunk and I was lighting a cigarette, so I didn't say anything. I was thinking about my father.

"Then I woke up," George said. He looked at Johnny, and Johnny looked down at the bar. He put the quarter in his pocket.

"You Catholic?" he asked my cousin. His voice was serious.

"Yes," George said, "Maronite Rite."

"I'm a Methodist," Johnny said, and he was serious. "I don't have dreams." He took the quarter from his pocket and put it in a jukebox selector near the cash register. The music came on loud, louder because the place was empty. The last waitress signed her time card, and Johnny put it in the cash drawer since it was the end of the pay-week. We watched her leave. Johnny stayed by the three sinks washing the empty mugs.

"Haleem," George was drunk now, too, "how old were you the first time?"

I said nothing. On purpose he did not look at me.

"When you first got lucky—" he lowered his voice and said the rest in Arabic, "with a woman, I mean."

Muskeen, I did not want to smile at this.

"Sixteen? Eighteen?"

"Twenty-three," I said.

He thought about this. Twenty-three. Was I lying to him? That was only three years ago, and I was still in the navy.

"Haleem," he said in Arabic, low so that Johnny would not hear, "how does one find a woman?"

I lit another cigarette. It would be wrong to make a joke of this.

"Jorgi," I said in Arabic, "such things will come with time." He waited. We were both drunk, and these were not the right words. But I could not say, The women will not have you because of the way you are, because you are *muskeen.*

"Jorgi," I said in English, "it happened to me the

first time when I least expected it, when I wasn't even thinking about it." This was true.

"It bothers me," he said.

"Nothing like that will happen if you try too hard."

"It bothers me, Haleem."

"Then listen," I said, and he leaned in close, "if it's that bad, then take twenty dollars and go buy it." I fell into Arabic. "There is no shame in that. Believe me, there is no shame."

George sat back against the bar. "I just might do that," he said, as if I had just told him to swallow a bottle of sleeping pills.

*

"We are all damned fools," my father used to say. In the middle of one night when I was a child, my father came from my mother's bedroom in his long-john underwear. He looked into the bathroom where I was sitting on the toilet. I'd had the cramps that evening, and my mother gave me a laxative before bed. He looked at me a moment, and I looked back at him, helpless. "We are all damn fools," he said and went into his own room next to the kitchen and shut the door. To have a father when you are nearly thirty, this is my wish. I was a damn fool to give George such advice, and he was a damned fool himself to even think about such advice, much less try to take it.

It was no more than a week after I talked with George in the tavern that he tried to buy a woman. With forty-some dollars in his pocket he got in his Chevy and drove to a motel near town that even today has a shady reputation. But he did not go in. He sat in the car with his motor running for half the night and, I suppose, scared hell out of the poor women inside who must have thought he was the police.

But I did not know about any of this until several years later. I saw only a little of George at the time because I was very busy with the things in front of me,

nearing thirty, smoking too much, visiting almost daily with my father in Calvary Cemetery.

It was in April or late March when George drove home from that motel in the middle of the night. And I found out later that it was around this time that he began counting his breaths per minute, worrying about how his heart skipped before he fell asleep. At night he sometimes had dreams in which everything was a jumble and he was sick in his sleep. Once he fainted while he was having Sunday dinner. His mother called me, and I drove him to Mercy's emergency room. The doctors put George in a private room, they took tests and examined him for almost a week. When he was released, I came in his Chevy to drive him home. Doctors Bain and Warren, who took care of our family after Doctor Binatti died, gave George some pills to calm him down. They told him to stop listening to his heart's beats, that it would beat even if he didn't want it to. They told him not to worry about his breathing, that his breath would come and go, come and go again. One young doctor, an intern from Argentina who was standing by the door till the others had left, touched George's shoulder and told him that, every now and then, he ought to get himself a woman. George only nodded his head, then followed me to the Chevy.

George went on, he went back to work in the restaurant, made up the classes he had missed at school. When he realized he was listening too closely to his heart, he took a pill; and he took another when he found himself counting his breaths per minute.

In May of that year, which was 1964, there was a party for Jiddo Braheem. The old ones got drunk and started singing. Soon they were crying about those who had died. And when one of them told about how Rasheed would laugh at a good joke, if it was told well, I left the room. I went into the kitchen to sit alone, for I

was a little drunk, too. George was there by the sink, fumbling with his bottle of pills.

I did not return to school the September after my father died and George went into the hospital. The university placement service found me a job with a discount firm in Pennsylvania. I emptied out my room above Uncle Habeeb's supermarket and loaded the car. My mother stood on the front porch when I came to say good-bye, and she gave me her blessing as I pulled out of the driveway.

Through an occasional letter and, more often, a long distance call, I kept in touch with George and the rest of the family. But I did not return for a visit, not for Christmas, not even for the funeral of Jiddo Braheem the Green Devil, who died that winter. I met an American woman, Sheila, and we were married before spring. My family did not know until after the ceremony, and so no one came. Sheila and I lived together two years and were divorced just before I reached thirty. The family felt it was bad to marry an American, but they felt that divorce was worse. My mother stopped writing, and George, busy with his senior year, wrote less and less often. Alone in the room I rented from a Polish woman, I reached thirty, and passed thirty. And one evening in late spring, on a day an unexpected storm had snowed across Ohio and Pennsylvania, I began drinking alone in my rented room. I toasted George's health and Jiddo Braheem's funny dance and the laughter of my father. I drank too much and almost took too many sleeping pills at once.

My Polish landlady found me. She called the rescue squad and she called my family in Ohio. At the hospital I got a telegram saying that Uncle Yousef, who feared airplanes, was on his way in a Greyhound. The afternoon I was released Uncle Yousef and I got drunk together and, for the last time, I wept for my father, who

45

had been dead for over five years. Uncle Yousef wept a little himself. Walking back to the hotel, he told a joke, and I told him the story of the rabbi and the priest. We both laughed because the story is a good one. *Ibn Rasheed,* he called me when he heard me laugh, the son of my father. The next day, while the snow began falling again, we boarded a bus together and came home.

We traveled in the snow and it was snowing when we arrived. George met us at the terminal. He looked a little leaner, his face showed its age more. He kissed me on the neck the way the older men do, and he laughed. There was a dinner waiting at Aunt Afifie's. The whole family was waiting. We packed my things in the trunk of the old Chevy. Uncle Yousef sat up front with George and I got in back. We passed Walbridge Park on the way. The snow was still falling, and the yellow crocuses and daffodils in the park were bowed nearly double under the weight of it. "Look at that," Uncle Yousef said, nodding his head toward the flowers and the snow. "Goddamn it."

*

With time, less than a year's time after that drive home and the happy, noisy meal at Aunt Afifie's, George fell in love with an American woman, and she with him. This happened when he least expected it. It happened with time. George held his peace and, trying not to think of his heartbeats, the breaths he took, the laughter of our dead ones, he married her. With time I married again, another American. The family received our wives, but not easily. After all, they were Americans. They could not make *phtire* or *tabouli,* and they both cringed at the sight of raw liver with onions. My wife tried to make *kibbee* once, but it turned to concrete in your stomach. So, to this day George and I eat egg salad sandwiches at family picnics. "The *kibbee* is not important," we tell the others, and they shake their heads to see us eat the egg salad. Some of the old ones think George and

I are somehow odd, a little funny. Crazy was the way
Aunt Afifie put it one day in Walbridge Park. This was
in April of 1969, only a short time after my wedding.
My Uncle Abd'Allah began playing the lute and his sons
beat time on the little Arab drums. Uncle Yousef took
out his handkerchief and led the *debkee*, slow, as it
should be led at first. Even the little children joined the
dance, slow, holding their excitement for when things
would become dizzy and stamping. I stood up and took
my wife's hand. In front of the picnic table I showed her
the basic steps, and she tried to follow them, watching
my feet, stumbling, laughing. George and his wife
watched us. Then George did a wonderful thing. He
threw down his egg salad sandwich and he stood up,
and his wife stood up with him. The four of us locked
arms. I showed them the steps as best I could. Then,
with our arms locked, we broke into the dance and
joined it. The snake became a circle, things got dizzy, we
were stamping. "Crazy Americans," Aunt Afifie said as
we spun past her. "Goddamn. Crazy people."

*

What I am telling has to do with fathers and dancing,
with death and little brothers. It comes from a time
when I walked with wet shoes through the parks of
Ohio or Pennsylvania and watched the snow fall down
on flowers in the late spring; a time when, nearing thirty
and miraculously passing thirty, I found myself able to
curse the late and unexpected snow, to curse it a short
curse and then hold my peace. For I knew – learned almost in fear – that the time had come for flowers, that
soon, this weekend or the next, people would come back
to the parks to picnic, to play, to laugh at jokes and
dance – especially dance. The yellow flowers, covered
and dripping, would die; but I knew that for now winter
was dead. I knew, whether I liked it or not, the time had
come for flowers.

Something Else

Aunt Rosa walks too slowly down the steps of old Saint Elias Church. Her wedding dress is yellow in the yellow light. People are throwing rice, their arms going slowly up and down again, and the rice falls slowly, white clouds suspended, then straight lines down. All this in silence. It is long ago, and there is only the whir and click of the projector.

"Rosa," Uncle Naseeb says.

In the middle of winter here is sunlight and the green grass of past times. The dead are alive again.

"There, Tonia." It is Aunt Helen's voice. "There's your father."

"Where?" Tonia sits forward and tilts her glasses so she can see better. Many of these films are familiar, but some she is seeing now for the first time.

"In the crowd," Aunt Helen says. "Now he's moving away. You can still see his hand, there, in the corner."

"God give him rest," Mama says.

The camera moves again, and in the upper corner of the screen Tonia can see her father's arm waving in slow motion, tossing rice; now part of his face, the nose and glasses, the little moustache.

"And God forgive him his sins," Mama continues,

48

blessing the screen with three fingers and the sign of the cross.

Tonia lights a cigarette and sits back, happy amid the warm confusion of voices. Never mind Mama. Since Uncle Naseeb thinks that this is Tonia's last night in Toledo, the end of a visit home, he has got the old projector working again especially for her.

Tomorrow Wayne, her husband, will drive up from Tulsa to take her back, and she will have to tell him that she is not going back with him. This is something she is certain of now, decided not during these three weeks at home, but before the visit even began, immediately and without reflection, on the morning of her departure; a decision confirmed in the hugs and kisses of the relatives who had come to greet her at the airport. No, she will not leave and go back with him.

In the morning she will tell Wayne that, simply, things had not been what she thought they would be, not what she had expected. She will say that she was too young and did not know her mind; she will mention Tulsa, so far from the family, and the settling down there into a day-to-dayness that made her fear for what would happen to the rest of her life.

Because even at the wedding it was normal (she will not tell him this), so normal and ordinary in spite of the things that were meant to make it seem special: the gold brocaded vestments of the priest, the flowers and rented tuxedos, incense, the reciting of vows. Almost five months ago, and she remembers clearly the sinking dread of that moment.

Later, there gradually came a sadness, dull and leaden, worsening over the weeks until one sleepless night when she gave way to tears and, strangely, to thoughts of her father. All that night Wayne hovered over her, putting his arms around her as she sat in the bedroom rocker, and she pushing his arms away; a night

that ended in morning and exhaustion and Wayne agreeing that, yes, maybe she ought to go home for a visit, if it would make her feel better.

Tomorrow she will have to tell him. And it will be over. Maybe the Church would even grant an annulment, seeing that they were married only five months, and that she was so young, now only just turned eighteen. But all this tomorrow. She puts out her cigarette. Tonight she wants to see her father again.

The action speeds, the camera jerks back to Aunt Rosa, and suddenly nothing is right. The film runs too fast: kisses become pecks and hugs are short grabs. There is laughter in the room. Little Alex is laughing harder than he should—even he knows that—but he does not know how to stop properly. "Aw, c'mon Alex," Naseeb, his father, says to help. "Finish it." He says this last gently, in Arabic.

The bride smiles at the room in trembling yellow, then orange light. The branches of the trees behind her are vibrating as if in an earthquake.

She is living in Detroit now.

"Seven children now, or eight?" Uncle Naseeb asks his wife. Rosa is her sister.

"Eight," Aunt Helen says.

"God help her," someone says.

There is a short, thick snore. Behind the screen Uncle Iskandar is asleep in a stuffed chair. His mouth would be open, as usual, his chin almost touching his chest. He would be asleep if there were no film and all the lights of his brother's large house were burning. He once fell asleep with a hand around a beer can and the other in a bag of potato chips. They took a photograph.

The camera pans the crowd once more, orange light deepening to red—a sign that the reel is almost ended. People wave. Again Tonia sees Papa's hand, the arm and shoulder in red light, a cheek and the little moustache. Then the film runs to white and upside-down numbers.

The lights are turned on while Uncle Naseeb changes reels, checking the labels for dates and their order. In the kitchen Mama helps with the coffee. Tonia can hear her in there, telling the other women about Papa and how in the old country her parents had first arranged for him to visit and have Turkish coffee. Tonia has heard it before; she knows her mother's stories, how they can change with the telling.

Mama did not marry Papa for love, that part never changes. She had told Tonia what it was like in Damascus. "He was unschooled, a stranger, as old as my father," Mama had said. "And I was young and pretty. It was shameful, a sin on my mother's head."

Tonia had seen the brown photographs. The dresses were old-fashioned, and there was the funny way Mama wore her hair, but the face was pretty, made up like a movie star's, and she was slim.

"And young!" Mama said. "This one was when we were just married. Look at me, almost a child. Even so, I was educated. And look at him there next to me. A villager. A mountain man."

". . . From the mountains, yes, but rich," Mama's mother had said. "Azar Yakoub has been to America."

"Then let him marry an *Amerkani*."

"Poor man, who would want an *Amerkani?*"

"If gold is cheap in America, why is he here?"

"So that he can take you there."

"I have heard him curse."

"Only when he forgets himself," Mama's mother said. "After all, he is a man. . . . "

So it was never love, even in the beginning, and later it was something else; it was Mama sitting alone in the dark of the kitchen saying her rosary, and Papa with his shoes off in the front room tired after standing all day at the cash register, offering Tonia dimes to curse in Arabic.

"Say *Blood descend upon you!*" he would tell her

and hold up a dime. "Say *Death open its mouth for you!*" and he would laugh to hear her parrot him in her little voice; and even when she failed, stuttering over *Nu'tah takhdaq* or *Y'hariq deen beyek akrut!* or the name of the angel of pain, *Izraieen,* Papa would still give her a dime.

*

Aunt Helen serves coffee and sesame cakes. Afterward, at a signal from his father, Little Alex pulls the chain of the small table lamp. The screen brightens, and it is Uncle Naseeb's back yard. The old barn is there, torn down now and replaced by the two-car garage. This too is old film; the grass is greener than real, the sunlight somehow dark.

Near the rose tree Aunt Helen is broiling skewered lamb meat over the charcoal. Uncle Naseeb puts his arms around her and they smile clownishly into the camera.

"Iskandar must have taken this one."

There is no response from the darkened room. Having finished his coffee and sesame cake, Uncle Iskandar is evidently asleep once more.

A little girl runs between Uncle Naseeb and Aunt Helen and makes a face in the camera. It is Tonia ("Look at you then!") in cowgirl outfit and glasses, her dark hair curly beneath the white hat. Behind them Papa is sitting in a lawn chair. He, too, is showing off, making a face for the camera. It is the same face. His lips move in Arabic: *Come here, My Heart.* Tonia runs to his side. The camera follows. Mama, thinner back then, stands behind the chair, and they pose. Papa reaches his arm up and tries to pull Mama down for a kiss. She twists away, arms waving, mouth working silently, and almost walks smack into the camera. Papa looks after her. Then his eyes narrow in sarcasm. He exaggerates a hand-to-breast pose and his lips move: *Return to me, O Beloved, my Sweet One, my Fragrant One!*

Uncle Naseeb still laughs the same way; on the screen he puts one hand to the side of his face, as he does now, looking at himself and laughing.

Not at all the way Papa used to laugh, loud and open-mouthed. His moustache was only a little wider than Charlie Chaplin's. He wore glasses. He was dark-skinned and short and heavy around the middle, like a mountain villager.

"You are your father's daughter," Mama told her once when she was still very little and dreaming of cow-girls. "You will grow up to be just like him."

"Just like him, Mama?"

"Already I see him in you, his eyes, his forehead. You have his hair, not mine."

Papa's hair was curly and coarse under the knit cap he wore even to bed.

Tonia did not want that. What she wanted was the tall cowgirl with smooth blonde hair, also named Tonia, who came to her imagination before sleep and stayed sometimes into her dreams. Her outfit was white, the hat and blouse and fringed skirt. The horse she rode was jet black except for the tail and mane, which were white. Of it all, that horse was the hardest to imagine—its mane would not stay pure white as she wanted it, or its coat would gradually turn brown like the milk horses that came by every morning. And the name, too, would change. For a while the horse was called Thunderbolt, which eventually became Tommy; Black Star, then sim-ply Blackie. No matter which she decided on, it would always—as if of its own accord—turn into something or-dinary: Magic to Mickey.

Papa was busy at the cash register when Tonia told him about the horse—its speed and intelligence, its fan-tastic colors. He only laughed and said yes, yes. Uncle Is-kandar, idly puffing a cigar laughed too. Just over five feet tall, he sat perched on an olive keg with shoes barely touching the sawdust. While he waited for Papa to close

up he began explaining to Tonia the palomino and the pinto, how most horses are either chestnuts or bays, or black with maybe a white foot or two.

Uncle Iskandar was a bookie—which she knew to be a kind of gambler—so horses were part of his business. Accordingly, his words took on for Tonia the incontestable authority of a businessman's.

"An all-black horse with one white foot is good luck," Uncle Iskandar said "so you put your money on him." And he added that Mickey was not a good name for a horse. "That is the name of a mouse," he said.

After that the horse was even harder to imagine, requiring effort now, concentration.

"Just like him, Mama?"

"And your mouth. He has taught you to say it all." Mama was not crying now. She sat next to the radio with a cold washcloth on her forehead. "And your belly, look how it is already."

Tonia looked down at herself, and Mama was right. So, she would be fat, too. She would be short. And wear glasses, and have a moustache like Papa. There was no other way. So, like the horse, the cowgirl would be no good anymore—short and fat and four-eyed, her upper lip black like a villain or a clown.

*

There is Aunt Helen, her hair black and shining in those days. She stands in the driveway next to Naseeb's old Packard, holding a handkerchief to her eyes.

"I'm crying there," Aunt Helen says. "What was I crying about?" She puts down her coffee cup. "When was that taken?" No one in the room remembers, and the only answer is a particularly full-bodied snore from Uncle Iskandar in a chair by the door.

"Wow!" Little Alex calls out in mock surprise, and everyone laughs.

Even Tonia laughs. Papa used to snore, and he and Mama were all the time arguing about it. Or they would

argue about something else. One night Tonia lay in bed listening to the two of them. He was cursing and Mama kept shushing him.

A low sound welled up in Tonia's throat as she listened. She struggled against it but it was no use. She took air and wailed.

The voices softened then fell silent. Papa came into the room.

"I had a bad thought," she said.

"Nothing. A dream." His face was black against the light from the open doorway. "Don't be afraid."

She sat up. "Papa, will I grow up to be like you?"

"Tch." He clicked his tongue – Arabic for *no* – and cocked his head as if to say, "Whoever heard of such a thing?"

"When I grow up, are you going to be my husband?"

"Tch."

"Then who?"

"A young man. Tall and young, with a red face like the French. He will put his arm around you," he circled her shoulders with one arm, "and you will go away with him."

"I won't."

Papa darkened. "There is no other way."

The film switches abruptly, after a rough splice, to what looks like the early sixties and one the Yakoub family reunions at Walbridge Park. Once more there is Aunt Helen. Only now instead of crying she is laughing again. And she is much older after the splice, grown suddenly gray. Tonia, too, is laughing at whatever it is that's so funny. She is not yet out of grade school, and already her baby fat is gone and she is almost as tall as Aunt Helen.

The camera swings slowly and takes in the others: young people far off by the park pavilion dancing the *debkee*-snake; closer, old women sitting at cards, the

tubes of water pipes dangling from their lips; old men in white shirts and suspenders, laughing into the camera, smoking cigars, cutting lamb shoulder roasts into small cubes. Papa leans forward in the old blue wheelchair, a cigar sticking straight out of his mouth. He does not know the camera is there.

Uncle Naseeb sighs. "This is the summer before he went back in the hospital."

Papa turns slowly, like one who senses he is being watched. His brown eyes look bigger than Tonia remembers them.

"Look how he lost weight," Aunt Helen says.

There is recognition, then anger. His lips move in Arabic: A blood clot choke you! and he hides his eyes with one hand.

In September of that same year, Mama invited a new parish priest to the house for dinner. Tonia wheeled Papa to the dining room and left him at the head of the table. Father Lascatta stood at the other end, waiting for Mama to come in from the kitchen. His hair was an ashy blond and he wore it neatly trimmed, flat on top in a style that was called the ivy league. Just like any other young man, Tonia thought.

She watched as he blessed the food. He had been ordained in May, so, she figured, he must be no more than twenty-six. Four years of college, four of seminary. Sister Gemma said that Jesuits study longer, but he was a regular priest and not a Jesuit. Still, more than twice her age.

Tonia glanced down. His shoes were different from the old-fashioned tie-ups the other priests wore. His were black loafers with leather tassels. Just like any other young man's shoes.

He finished the blessing and they sat down. Mama had made a special dish that day, *ghammeh* – sheep tripe stuffed with rice and pine nuts and simmered in a doughy sauce – which Tonia hated not for its taste so

much as for the way it looked, grayish white, bulging glossy on the plate. Father Lascatta said he'd never seen anything like it before. He was Italian on his father's side only. His mother was part French and part something else. Papa laughed at that. He laughed even more when Father said that he spoke neither Italian nor French, only English.

"Oh, and Latin, too," Father said, winking at Tonia. She squirmed in her chair and giggled. His eyes were brown. In the summer he had a suntan.

After dinner they had coffee, laughing at Father's stories about the seminary and the old priests who taught there. When things fell quiet, Papa leaned forward—like a merchant talking business to another merchant—and asked why God in His mercy sent him *this*; he slapped the arm of the wheelchair.

Embarrassed, Mama hurried by them into the kitchen.

"Well, Azar," Father Lascatta smiled as he looked down into his empty cup. It seemed strange to Tonia that such a young man should call Papa by his first name. Then Father looked up, not smiling, and he told about his own father who had had such terrible arthritis that he used to chew aspirins at the breakfast table. Papa said, "That's just exactly what I'm talking about," and Father Lascatta looked as if he did not know what to say. He said, "God gives suffering to those He loves most."

These words, the slow way he said them, gave Tonia gooseflesh. She began to picture herself in a nun's habit. A crown of thorns—

"Love!" Papa said in Arabic. "Urine from the Black Dog drown such love!"

*

He died the following November, two days before Tonia's twelfth birthday. The smell of flowers made the air in the funeral home thick, as oppressive as the first-

time hugs of distant relatives, the scratchy men's kisses on the neck.

Before the casket was closed, the people filed by for a final glance. It was a fast line; some did not even look. A woman from the mortuary staff began to sing a song about sleeping and dying, and this started everyone weeping. Even Uncle Naseeb wept, who in his tears said such devices were shameful and cheap. Tonia and Mama knelt before the casket. She looked at her father's hands, then at the made-up face with its calm, almost-smile he never smiled in life. All his life he was not calm. Only the hair in his ear looked like him. He should have a cigar in his mouth. And he should be cursing all of them.

The woman stopped singing. Tonia bent over, as Mama had done, and kissed Papa's cheek. It was not Papa's cheek. They closed the casket. Mama cried out, and Uncle Naseeb and Uncle Iskandar had to hold her, although it was never love.

It was normal. He was sick for a long time, he died. Normal despite candles and flowers, purple vestments, incense, and the altar sodality all kneeling together for the rosary.

This made Tonia afraid, seeing her father so easily and so truly gone. Later, the comforting words of the nuns at school took their effect, Father Lascatta's words in the confessional, and she came to believe that what had happened was not normal but special, the welcoming of a soul into heaven.

She was a child, she believed them. And years later, flourishing the diamond and fussing over the selection of bridesmaids' dresses, she must have been a child then, too; she had tried to make it all seem so special. It was not. Of course not—for even then, in the very effort of her excitement, she had known that it was really only normal, as ordinary as, after all, the death of her father had been ordinary.

*

Uncle Naseeb puts on a new reel that has not been labeled. The colors are true and the motion normal. It is new film, taken just over a year ago on the grounds of the courthouse downtown. A congressional candidate is making a speech. In the crowd, Tonia and Wayne are holding hands. She does not take her eyes off him. He is tall, fair, his nose and forehead reddened by the sun. In his free hand he holds a cigarette.

"When he comes tomorrow," Aunt Helen says as the camera moves closer to Wayne, "tell him I got *kibbee* and grape leaves waiting for him. When do you think he'll be here?"

"Early." Tonia answers without taking her eyes from the screen. "He's leaving right after work."

"Straight through? What's his hurry?"

"Never mind, Helen," Uncle Naseeb says.

"Driving all night—"

"Helen."

Tonia smiles, eyes still on the screen. Then the camera swings back to the candidate, his mouth moving so fast no one can read his lips.

"Save your wind," an out-of-town cousin says to the screen. "You're going to lose anyway!"

("... It is not what you think it is," Mama had told Tonia. "It is something else, My Heart."

He was an American, and he was almost six years older than Tonia.

"Too soon, My Eyes."

She was only seventeen. His home and the job waiting for him were far away in Tulsa.

"Your father, God give him rest, would forbid this."

But since Tonia said they would run off if they had to, and since, after all, Wayne was a Catholic, Mama went downtown with them to sign her name. . . .)

The film runs through a splice, and there is Wayne again, talking now to Michael Rakosi, his friend who'd

come all the way from New York to be best man. The moustache Wayne grew for the wedding is blond and barely visible in this light. The two of them, nervous in tuxedos, turn to the camera and pose.

And now the church aisle, lit by bar-lamps to unnatural brightness. In the laced and buttoned dress, Tonia looks like the old pictures of Mama. Uncle Naseeb gives her away to Wayne. They kneel before Father Lascatta, who has grown noticeably paunchy now even under the flowing white vestments, his hair and sideburns grown long with the fashion. Everyone is smiling. Outside, Tonia's eyes are wide, almost frantic as she looks at Wayne. He puts his arm around her shoulders and, hunching against the rice, they run toward the camera.

Afterward at the reception, the band played a medley of Irish songs for Wayne's family, although he is only part Irish. Tonia sang with them.

*

The lamps are lit, and little Alex takes a dish of mints around the room. Some have stood up already, getting purses and coats. Mama is telling a story about the time they lived in the rooms behind Papa's first store. Tonia remembers. When she was five they moved from there to Mulberry Street. Not long after the move, Papa first began getting sick. ("A black dog," he told Tonia during one of his hospital stays, "must have urinated on our doorpost the night we moved in. Why, My Bones? Because that is when my bad luck began." Then he cursed the house on Mulberry Street, cursed the truck that moved them there.)

"This man worked for us," Mama is saying, "driving deliveries, and he knew that Azar put the store money in his pants pocket at night."

The screen is taken down and put away in the hall closet. Uncle Naseeb listens to Mama while he rewinds the reels.

"This one," Mama nods toward Tonia, "was asleep next to me."

She was not asleep. It is one of Tonia's earliest memories. She had been sick in the night, and Mama had got in bed to comfort her.

"I woke up and I saw him bending over the bed. He was reaching for my rings. I screamed 'Azar! Azar!' and I stuck my hands like this." Mama puts down the coffee cup and shows them, crossing her arms to hide her hands in her armpits.

Tonia remembers the man's face shadowed in the bedroom darkness, the pearly gray hat and the finger over the lips. *Shh, lady, shh*, he kept saying, *Please lady, shh*. As his voice became more frantic, Tonia huddled closer to Mama.

"He said, 'Shut up, lady!' Then he hit me on the head and ran out. This one here, she slept through the whole thing."

Tonia says nothing. She smiles at little Alex and takes a mint.

"I went into our room, and what was Azar doing? He was snoring like an elephant."

One of the out-of-town cousins shakes his head and starts chuckling. Uncle Naseeb smiles as if he has heard the story before.

"I shook Azar awake and he told me to stop screaming, that I was embarrassing him in front of the neighbors. 'Hoost! Hoost! you had a nightmare,' he kept saying.

"So I put my hand in my hair and I show him my hand and the blood and I say, 'Azar, is this a dream?'"

Mama's face changes, her mouth tightens at one corner, her eyelids sag, and she almost looks like Papa.

"Azar sees the blood and he begins to shake his head this way and that way, like this, this way and that way, and he says 'Don't...ob...ob...be afraid...

ob...ob...ob...,' and he sits right down on the floor."

The out-of-town cousin is laughing so hard now — a wheezing, smoker's laugh — that his wife has to slap him on the back. When he had caught his breath, Mama turns in her chair and tells the rest to him.

"Azar slept in his long underwear, see, and the cap on his head all the time? Well, he sits down in his long underwear, and then he lies down, 'Ob...ob...don't...be...ob...,' then he puts his hands straight out and he faints! So I have to carry this one in my arms and walk two doors down to call the police myself!"

The laughter is so loud and so sudden that Uncle Iskandar lurches awake in his chair, blinking left and right. Tonia smiles but does not join in. Her eyes burn.

The others, noticing something amiss, fall silent. Then Mama stands up. She reaches for her purse, and the moment passes. There are kisses and hugs, promises to come back and invitations to come over and see us, too.

"You tell Wayne I cooked special for him!" Aunt Helen says.

*

Late into the night Tonia lies open-eyed in the familiar darkness of her old bedroom on Mulberry (in the house where Papa had no luck, its doorpost wetted by a black dog), and she tries to bring back the face, the glasses and the little moustache. The features will not fix. Even the tilt of his head will not stay right. It is no use.

Despite the prayers and candles and talk of heaven, so normal after all, so really and truly dead. No matter if remembered this way or that way, always made into something else. There is no other way. She closes her eyes.

The horse is running fast in yellow light, a jet black horse, its mane and tail pure white.

Outside there is the sound of wind. Normal after all

—the rice and champagne toasts, the honeymoon and the life after, the children to come, the picnics and re-unions and funerals to come. Wayne to come. This min-ute on the highway somewhere amid the rush of wind in the car vent; the way he drives, fast, one arm around her shoulders. Yes, and she with him. That too, normal. There is no other way.

News from Phoenix

After three years in America, Isaac's mother was still afraid of Jews. Damascus remained fresh in her, the dark evenings huddled with her sisters, fearful and giggling around the brazier while her uncle told stories. He was an archimandrite in the Maronite Church, and even now Sofia trembled at the thought of him. His cassock reeked sweat and incense, and she remembered, too, the thick bitter smell of the Turkish anise drink he favored, how his beard glistened oil as he sipped—and such stories! No! She put both hands to her ears and shouted at her husband: "Amos!"

Who paid no attention. It was closing time, and Isaac's father stood at the cash register counting money. His lips made the quick, breathy sounds of numbers.

"Amos, they are Jews!" she shouted. "Jews!" as if that word said it all, and anyone who had an ounce of sense would understand.

Isaac was almost six years old and he had heard her stories, her uncle the archimandrite's stories, of what Jews did to little Christian children, of throats slit and blood taken for secret ceremonies, the children found white and limp in the morning, thrown into some alley behind the weavers' market or the gold *souq*. Even so, he did not understand. (What had Charlotte and Erwin Klein to do with all that?) But he became frightened

anyway. Somehow there had been danger in the ride downtown for ice cream and the little gifts Charlotte had bought. He and his brother had just had a narrow escape, that much he understood, and he began to cry. Then Demitri, younger than Isaac by three years, took his thumb from his mouth and gave out that slow, toneless wail of his that understood nothing except that Isaac was crying.

"Hoost!" The sound came from their father, and immediately the boys fell silent. "*Izraiyeen* take you!" Amos cursed his wife with the angel of death. He slapped the money into the cash drawer. "Look how you're scaring them—why?" His voice was big, although he was not yet shouting. That would come. "Give them back the toys." He wiped his hands across the belly of his apron and waited.

Sofia lowered her eyes. Then, whispering a prayer against the Evil Eye, she handed the package of crayons to Isaac and the balsa wood airplane to Demitri.

"Hoost!" Amos said again. She turned away, but her lips continued to move, silently, as little as the syllables of the prayer would allow.

Demitri tossed the airplane, and the four of them watched it float up in a gentle arc. It banked just shy of the flypaper that hung in coils above the butcher block, hesitated, then dropped abruptly into a banana crate.

"G'wan now," Amos said in English. "G'wan, take da ara-blane downstairs."

They obeyed, Demitri following Isaac into the cellar. Beneath the stairs was the toilet stool. Isaac nudged the lid down with his toe, then sat listening to the voices above while his brother threw and chased the airplane among the racks of empty soda pop bottles. His father's shouting, when it came, would be full of curses, but it would be brief. Afterward a silence would fall between them, stiff with exaggerated politeness; and in the silence his curses—of blood, of lineage and the womb that

gives issue—would hover above the tiny store and the flat upstairs until finally, through small familiar signals of regret, Amos took them back one by one.

And the two of them would have something warm to drink then, they always did. Sofia lit the gas burner and stirred the base of the Turkish samovar around and around in the flame, adding anise seed in pinched doses until its strong licorice smell filled the kitchen, and still Amos would say "More...more," and she would add another pinch, and yet another. The yellow brew, called *yensoun*, remained syrupy even after it settled. Amos drank it that way. Into her own cup Sofia first spooned plenty of sugar, and when she poured for herself she poured *yensoun* and cream at the same time, two-handed, lest the cream curdle in the strong brew.

Sometimes Isaac asked for a taste, but always they told him no, that it was too strong for children, and they would send him out of the kitchen. So he would sit in the front room and listen to the silence dissolve between them, Sofia gazing into the dregs of Amos's cup and finding journeys there, money, business for the store, news from a friend. Her voice would grow high, child-like with foretelling, and soon Amos would be laughing.

Because, after all, his wife wasn't a mean woman. He told people that. More like a child, he told them, she believed everything. Blood and secret ceremonies—an uncle's bogeyman stories! And would an archimandrite, in the Latin rite equal to a monsignor, tell such horrors to a child? Probably not. Probably she simply remembered the stories that way, adding his authority to them later, as children sometimes do; and who would curse a child? Especially one so often ignored, left to herself here in a tiny flat above a tiny store, surrounded by taverns and pawnshops and the blue-eyed bums asking for wine. America was hardly what a child must have expected it to be. A child, he told people, given to petulance when things were boring, when the weather was hot and there was nothing to do.

*

Isaac pressed his nose to the doorscreen and stared at the way the air wiggled between buses and trucks and automobiles when there was a red light. Too hot for business, his father had said. Amos was sitting behind the counter with his cousin Milad, playing a hand of *baserah*. There had been no customers for hours. Sofia stood at the display window with a piece of newspaper, fanning herself and Demitri, who stood close by her despite the heat. It was quiet in the store, only flies and the rustle of paper. Now and then Uncle Milad would mutter something at his cards—Arabic or English, it was hard to tell with the cigar in his mouth.

"But there is nothing to do in this country!" Sofia shouted as if in the middle of an argument. Isaac started at the suddenness of her voice. The men looked up. Amos kinked an eyebrow but said nothing, and after a moment Milad gathered the cards and began shuffling them.

"The children! Poor things, look how they have nothing to do."

"Take them to the park," Amos said. He nodded for Milad to deal.

"I do not know the buses."

Milad dealt, and the men studied their cards.

"I do not know the buses," she said again. "You must come with us."

Amos glared up at her. Even Isaac understood: customers or no, business is still business.

Have they been to the *arta muzeem?*" Milad asked.

"Truly," Amos said, "take them to the *ara muzeema*."

"What is that?"

"It is free. They have pictures on the walls. You can go look at the pictures."

"And sometimes music, too," Milad said. "Violins, pianos."

Sofia thought a moment.

"And in the summer," Milad added, *aira condition.*"

"Still, I do not know the buses."

"You do not have to change buses," Amos said. "It is right here on Monroe Street. That way, not even four kilometers."

"The driver will not understand me."

Milad put down the cards. "I will take them in my *machina.*"

"Sit down," Amos said. "It is your play."

Sofia knew only the Adams bus that went downtown and the Jefferson bus that brought her back. Her English was still terribly broken, even after three years; some said she wasn't trying to learn. Charlotte Klein had offered to drive her to a high school where English was taught at night, but Sofia refused to go. She wouldn't leave the children alone, she said. Also, Charlotte Klein was a Jew.

"Take the bus on the corner and say to the driver: *De ara muzeema,*" Amos said. "Sit behind him, and he will tell you when he reaches it."

"*D'Aram muzeema,*" Sofia sighed, then she put down the newspaper. "*D'arama amuzeema.*"

Amos gave her money from the cash drawer. "And dress up the boys," he said.

She washed Isaac and Demitri and had them put on the blue trousers with suspenders and the white shirts they wore for church. Then she packed a shopping bag with lunch.

When the bus arrived, Sofia told the driver several times but he still couldn't understand her. Finally, Isaac tried, speaking slowly and carefully, and the man appeared to understand. They sat behind the driver, Demitri moaning a little because he was still afraid of buses and the noise of traffic. While Isaac wasn't afraid, he could never seem to get used to the diesel smell that

buses had, nor the whine of gears building, but not enough, not quite enough, before the releasing lurch and hiss of the air brakes. It went on that way for blocks until at last the driver turned to them. "This is it," he said.

Sofia looked at him.

"Your stop, ma'am."

Sofia smiled.

"The art museum," the driver said. "Ar-rt mew-see-uhm."

Isaac understood first and took his mother's hand. But after the bus had moved away, leaving them on the sidewalk, they saw no art museum, no pictures on walls; only a hot summer confusion of streets and buildings and changing traffic lights. Although there were signs set low in the power-trimmed lawns, the words were meaningless to them. After a moment Sofia took a few steps in one direction, turned—the boys wheeling beside her in wide arcs—and started in another; then she stopped. She began to curse the art museum and the bus driver and Amos, too, using not the exact pronunciation of the profanity but changing a letter or a syllable, therefore cursing but not the words of cursing, not the words of anything, and so not a sin.

They crossed the street and waited for the homeward bus. But no sooner had they sat on the bench than they began to hear music from, it seemed, just around the corner. They listened to it a while. Finally, the return bus nowhere in sight, they picked up the shopping bag and turned the corner.

The music was coming from loudspeakers atop the roof of a small, white building. There were pictures painted on the walls and windows, bright cartoon shapes of blue and yellow and orange. Little plastic pennants flapped from wires. Above it all, high on a white post, was a painting of a red horse with wings.

Sofia and Isaac and Demitri sat down on the tiny

lawn in front of the place, took out their lunch—lamb meat patties, turnips pickled in beet juice, rolled grape leaves, olives, and cheese and fruit—and began to eat.

"*Aira condition,*" Sofia snorted. She fanned herself with a piece of waxed paper.

Automobiles drove onto the lot, and the attendants in spotless new uniforms immediately began polishing the windshields. Children pointed and laughed from back-seat windows. Someone in a green car, a woman or a young man, yelled "Hey, Gypsies!" as the car pulled into traffic. Sofia understood that word. She stood and cast a sign after the car—thumb and two fingers clenched, the fig—and shouted as she did so, forgetting to change the letters or the syllables. Sitting down again, she said a blessing to erase the curse.

A horn honked from the street behind them. The boys turned together; it was Charlotte and Erwin Klein. "Mama, mama!" Demitri shouted in the only English he knew. Sofia would not turn to look. "Hoost," she said. When Demitri began to move, she grasped him by the suspenders and pulled him down. Charlotte got out of her car, smiling as she always smiled whenever she saw Demitri. She bent over and spoke to Sofia in careful, distinct English. Isaac understood. She was offering them a ride home. Sofia also understood (that much Isaac could tell) but she opened her hands and shook her head no. "*Yahood,*" she said to Isaac and Demitri, *Jews,* so they would understand.

Charlotte was a small, very thin woman. She had straight hair, and Isaac thought it pretty just now how outdoor light changed it from blonde to almost red. Her eyes, however, weren't pretty at all. Magnified by glasses, they seemed too large for her face, and the harlequin slant of the frames made them look squinty. But Isaac never paid much attention to eyes; he would always remember hers as blue, maybe. It was mouths that he looked to. Tears or laughter or anger, for him it was

the turn of the mouth that each time signaled first, and not the eyes. (Once, when Amos had removed his belt and stamped after the boys as they cowered together in a corner, Isaac pulled loose of Demitri and said, "Papa, your pants are gonna fall down!" and he remembered how his father had stopped short, and, although his eyes never blinked even, one side of his mouth began working against the laughter. Twisting and clenching against it, before he dropped the belt and shuffled into the kitchen where Mama was already laughing.) Charlotte had a wide, full-lipped mouth, with that little bleb of flesh in the center of the upper lip that Isaac would forever like in a woman, associating it somehow with generosity and kindness.

Charlotte looked back at the car. She exaggerated a shrug, and Erwin waved her the come-on sign with his arm. Sofia continued to smile at all this as if she understood none of it. Charlotte talked a moment with Erwin at the car, then Erwin went inside the white building and stood at the pay phone in the window. When they drove away, Sofia was still smiling, looking straight ahead.

Only minutes passed before Milad pulled up in his ancient creaking automobile and told them to get in quickly, quickly. When they got home, Amos was furious.

*

The building where the Kleins lived and where Erwin Klein had his law office was within walking distance of the store, but toward downtown and away from the bums; an area where the streets began to be lined with trees and shrubs set in white half-barrels. Doormen wearing gold braid stood beneath scalloped marquees fringed with gold. The buildings they served housed expensive shops on the lower floors, as well as the offices of doctors, brokers, attorneys like Erwin Klein. From the paneled lobbies elevators carried residents to their apartments. One rainy afternoon Charlotte took the

boys up there with her, to the elegant quiet of her living room where Demitri was fascinated by his blue image in the blue-tinted mirror top of the coffee table.

She had no children. Married in her mid-thirties and resigned, it seemed, to never having them, she made Demitri her favorite. It was only natural; Demitri had the deep brown eyes that women liked, and his mile-a-minute Arabic must have sounded cute to an American. Demitri took to her as well, and soon she was driving him to the dimestore or the Saturday movies. Of course, Isaac went, too, so there would be no jealousy.

Sofia raised her voice against all this, "In their temple they learn the Evil Eye!" and Amos would blow up at her, "Think of it, a woman childless at her age, just think of it!" Then he would add, "You are no neighbor."

Two years ago when Milad Yakoub first sold the butcher shop to Amos, it was Erwin Klein who had taken care of the legal matters—the loan, the transfer of deed, licenses for beer and wine to carry out. "He understands business," Milad had told Amos in Arabic. "Trust him and keep your mouth shut." And so when Erwin advised that the name, "Yakoub Market," was worth something to the business, Amos kept his mouth shut and did not change the name of the store to his own. Later, when Erwin suggested a line of party products—soft drinks and packaged snack foods—Amos trusted the advice. He ordered from the wholesaler according to a list Erwin drew up for him, and he realized a profit and an increase in business.

"This one," Amos told the boys in English, "he is schooled," and he would raise one hand toward Erwin, indicating a respectful silence.

Erwin did look like a smart man; he had a high wide forehead, glasses, and a straight, even line of a mouth that could answer squarely to anything, or so it seemed to Isaac. He was very tall, too, and very, very skinny.

"He was sick probably all his life," was how Sofia saw it. "Probably his mother had thin milk." And indeed there was a kind of sickliness about him, even his laugh; you expected it to be bigger than it was. Nevertheless, he did laugh, breaking the respectful silence as he lifted Demitri up almost to the ceiling of the store. Then he would pick up Isaac, too, so there would be no jealousy.

In June of their third year in America, Amos received a letter from Saint Patrick School informing him that Isaac would not be admitted into the first grade. That same morning he took both boys and walked them hand in hand to the school. Two nuns who were standing in the foyer with their black bookbags made a fuss over Demitri, and Amos let them. Then he asked to see the nun whose signature appeared at the bottom of the letter.

She was an old woman with a quick, friendly smile, and yes, she remembered Isaac well. Several weeks before, she had observed him during a series of tests, how he'd fretted in tight-lipped defeat over nursery rhymes and geometric puzzles and even her own simple directions. So, when Amos began to explain that his son was bright and his only problem was that he didn't know English well enough yet since they almost never spoke it at home, her smile vanished. She interrupted him with a stiff shake of her head, no. Amos tried again—"Maybe, Mum, wit' the extra help," and "Maybe wit' special books,"—but the more he tried the more she seemed to grow impatient. Isaac could see it all in the set of her mouth. Finally, when his father asked to speak with the principal, her lips formed a rigid curve: *These people,* she was thinking. But she didn't want trouble, Isaac could see that too, and after a moment she signaled them to follow her down the polished halls to the office.

The principal must have been expecting them; she was adamant from the start. "This boy," she said, busily moving a sheaf of papers from one corner of her desk to

73

the other, "is simply not ready for first grade, at least not at Saint Patrick's." And that was all. An uneasy silence followed, then the principal stood up as if to dismiss them. But Amos remained seated, smiling; he was trying everything.

"Listen, Mum," he said, "I have a joke. . . ."

He usually tried this with customers when they complained about prices or the freshness of the meat. The joke was one of his funny ones, about the rabbi and the priest. Even so, the principal kept a stone face all through it; when it was ended, she was actually frowning.

Outside, Amos cursed both nuns by name, a short vicious curse concerning, as Isaac would always remember, nipples and squirting blood.

Then he brightened. He hitched his trousers and told the boys to wait for him here on the school steps while he went across the street.

Beyond the traffic Isaac saw a row of small shops. "What for, Papa?"

"What for? Telephone. Never mind what for!"

Isaac watched him go. He looked silly, hurrying off toward a phone booth in those large gray trousers, the butt-fold wagging left right left like a tail. But Isaac could not turn away from it; his eyes fixed themselves on that rear as it worked anxiously through the indifferent roar of Monroe Street for his sake alone. Poor butt; his father was trying everything.

When Amos returned, he gathered the boys to him and sat down on the steps beneath the principal's window. He began to sob loudly, all the time muttering curses and wiping his eyes with a red handkerchief, although Isaac could see that there was nothing to wipe. Now and then Amos would look up at the window, pause, then bury his face in Isaac's neck or Demitri's curls. At last the door opened, and soon Isaac was again

sitting with his brother in a corner of the principal's office.

She was still firm, but this time she spoke slowly, in little words, the way some people talk to bums. But this time it was Amos who interrupted. "I called up a friend onna telephone," he said. "Him he's gonna talk for me."

The principal sighed. "All right," she said, "all right."

Finally, Erwin Klein arrived. He had on sneakers and tennis shorts and a white v-neck sweater, but when he began talking everything changed. He spoke such perfect English—so rapidly Isaac could barely make it out—and with such confidence that he looked the principal directly in the eye. He didn't look sick at all that day. He was handsome without his glasses, sunburned on the cheeks and forehead, and skinny, yes, but so much taller than Amos. When he was finished, the principal's stone face had relaxed into a smile. "Well, yes," she agreed, "I suppose it's worth a try."

At that, Amos made an exaggerated, grateful bow. "*Kes umeek*," he said in Arabic, *Your mother's vulva*. She smiled. Demitri began to giggle, and she reached out and touched his curls the way a mother would. Isaac could see then that she wasn't a mean person, not really. She just didn't want trouble.

And so Isaac was admitted into the first grade. With the help of a novice nun who tutored him after school, his English improved greatly, and by the following June he would become one of the five gold-star readers in his class.

Amos showed his gratitude to the Kleins: the groceries he had delivered to their door were always wholesale. And even Sofia's protests began to diminish; eventually, she said nothing at all. It was in October of Isaac's first year of school that she told her husband

about the slowness she'd been noticing in Charlotte, a slight change in her walk, and the way her mind seemed to be on other things. Then, one night Sofia dreamed of a death, and she awoke laughing.

"Good news!" she said at breakfast. "Soon they will have their own."

"How?" Amos was still in his nightshirt.

"In dreams, death always means a birth."

"Who died?"

"Missus Charlotte—so it will be a boy. Think of it, they will have their own now."

"*Inshallah*," Amos said, *God willing.*

But even in the happiness of that moment, while his mother stirred the samovar of *yensoun,* clucking on like a nested pigeon, Isaac saw his father's eyebrow go up in doubt.

The doubt vanished one Saturday afternoon, only a week or so later, when Erwin stopped by the store. It seemed one of his usual after-lunch visits except that when he spoke his voice had a forced casualness to it. Finally, unable to mask his feelings any longer, he told Amos that Charlotte had seen the doctor and that, yes, it was certain.

Amos laughed. "Good news!" he said in Arabic, echoing Sofia's words. Then he leaned over the butcher block and muttered something that Isaac didn't catch, and both men began to laugh. Leaving Sofia to watch the store, Amos led Erwin into the back room and opened a bottle of Jewish wine with the star on it.

Less than a month later, the baby was born dead. When the phone rang with the news, Isaac was doing his after-school chores, carrying empty soda pop bottles down the basement stairs to sort them.

"Missus Charlotte!" Amos smiled. And forever in Isaac's memory of that day his father would be standing at the pay phone, smiling and listening, and his smile

fading. "No, Mum, he is not here. He was here after the lunch, but not now. Downtown, he tell me."

Sofia, too, had sensed something wrong. She put Demitri down from her lap and stood up.

"He don' say no more" – his voice was shaking now – "only downtown. No, Mum, I don' know where." He listened a moment more, then nodded his head quickly and hung up. Rushing, searching his pockets, talking to himself and to Sofia, he scooped some dimes from the cash drawer and ran back to the phone.

"Where?" Sofia asked.

"He's downtown! Where? Shut up! Downtown!"

Amos inserted a dime and dialed. "Quickly!" he said over his shoulder, but Sofia was already out the door. Isaac saw her pass the display window pulling on her coat as she hurried down the sidewalk in the direction of Charlotte's street.

A woman's voice came on the line. Amos was polite to her, but he could not keep his voice from shouting. Then there was Doctor Binatti's voice, big even over the phone.

Amos began in Arabic, caught himself, and started again in English. Then he noticed the boys, Isaac with pop bottles hanging from both hands, and he turned a little away and said the rest quietly into the receiver.

Hanging up, he said "Close your mouth," and Isaac closed his mouth.

A customer came into the store, then another. Demitri began to fuss, and Isaac took his hand and led him upstairs for a nap. When he returned, his father was slicing liver for the first customer's order. After a while, Isaac went down into the basement and used the toilet, remembering later to jiggle the handle. Then he continued sorting – Coke, Hires, Whistle, and Crush. He came up again at the sound of the back door, but it was not his mother, only one of the bums looking to earn wine

money. His father sent the man away; there wasn't any work. Later, Amos made liverwurst sandwiches. Demitri awoke from his nap, and they ate. Amos drank a beer after his sandwich. Sofia still was not back.

"G'wan, get out-a-side," Amos told the boys in English, but Isaac lingered in the back of the store. Demitri, eyes liquid and calm and understanding nothing, stayed by his brother.

When Sofia came in, her face was white. She sat on a stool behind the counter while Amos finished with a customer. She had been crying, and when she spoke she used Arabic so the customer would not understand. "Little, little," she began, so quietly that Isaac could barely make out the rest. "Small as my hand," she said, "but perfect." The customer left. Isaac crept toward the front so he could hear. "Perfect," Sofia said again. "Everything. It even had a little pee-pee."

Amos looked down and made a noise with his tongue, tch.

"And Mister Erwin?" he asked.

"He was downtown."

"Woman, I know that. Has he been told?"

She nodded. "He is there now. He is going with her to the hospital."

Amos made the sound again, tch.

"Even so, it is all as God would have it," Sofia said, and Amos looked at her. She smiled. "It did not die a Jew. While Doctor Binatti he was busy, I took water from the kitchen," she was not looking at his face, "and gave it baptism."

Amos turned away from her. "Watch the store," he said. He came to the back of the store and stood there a moment, looking down at the spattered sawdust beneath the butcher block. Then he noticed Isaac. Nudging the boy aside, he lifted a soda pop crate and carried it down into the cellar.

Isaac listened at the doorway. He could hear the roar

and suck of the toilet, its float frozen with rust. He heard his father lift the tank lid and adjust the valve. Then Isaac, too, picked up a soda pop crate.

Amos was standing before a row of bottle racks, head down, his arms loaded with bottles. He was sorting them. "Tch," he said when he heard Isaac behind him, but he did not send the boy away. After a minute, Sofia followed, carrying Demitri.

"What is it, Amos?" she asked, but he kept his back to her. "I shouldn't have?"

Amos turned around. Isaac could see that he was ready to blow up. Then it went out of his face. He sat down on a soda pop crate and put the bottles at his feet. "Is this how you watch the store? No matter." He spoke quietly. "No difference." Then he looked up, blinking into the lightbulb behind Sofia's head. "Go upstairs. Make *yensoun*," he said, his fingers dangling helpless among the bottles. "I want something warm to drink."

*

In December Amos phoned to invite the Kleins for Christmas Eve dinner. Although it was practically a last-minute idea ("So what if they are Jews," he told Sofia as he dialed, perhaps forgetting that the idea had been hers in the first place, "how can Christmas offend them?") the Kleins not only accepted, they arrived, like a bachelor uncle, two hours early. "Before the stores close," they explained, and they took the boys to a shopping center—Isaac unsure about seeing Santa, Demitri breathless with excitement—and brought them back loaded with gifts. They brought red wine with them, too, with the star on it, and after dinner sat drinking and talking, asking Sofia about the customs of Christmas in the old country. Then they told of a vacation they were planning to begin in January, an extended tour of the southwest and Mexico.

"To get away from Ohio's winter," Charlotte said. Isaac glanced briefly at Erwin. His face was pale, the

corners of his mouth pinched in. There was a brief silence, then Amos turned the talk to houses; he was seriously considering a place across town from the store. As he began to describe its two storeys, its yard, and its real neighborhood, far from the bums and broken glass, Sofia's face glowed.

Then Charlotte confessed that they, too, were looking to move, and that this was another reason for their trip. Phoenix had wonderful sunshine, she said, year round, and the — she paused — the facilities there had been highly recommended.

And it was then that Isaac began to sense that things were changing. Soon everything would be different, and somehow he would have to accustom himself.

Later, when the others were busy — Erwin putting together a toy ferris wheel for Demitri, Sofia busy with dessert — Charlotte and Amos sat down together on the couch and began to talk very quietly. Isaac didn't think it was right to listen on purpose.

"And if anything happens to him," Charlotte removed her glasses and put them back on again, "well, I don't know what I'll do." But she said it as if she did know what.

After dessert there was, of course, *yensoun*. Charlotte and Erwin exchanged glances, then laughed in disbelief at the third or fourth time Amos called out "More!" and Sofia added yet another pinch.

They laughed again, afterward, when Sofia began reading the cups — journeys and money and love. The drink must have heartened her; she told how her uncle the archimandrite had taught her to read cups, and when she began to describe the man himself ("Hees beard, it come down to here, an' my father he said you can comb a pounda grease outta it!") there was another peal of laughter.

But what if anything did happen? The thought came to Isaac amid the laughter, himself laughing. Erwin

looked so thin, sitting back from the table now, balancing the tiny cup and saucer on the bone of his knee. And if anything did happen, then the news, when it came, would come from Phoenix.

Turning to the stove, Isaac took the samovar in one hand, the creamer in the other, and poured himself a cup as he'd seen his mother do it, two-handed. If she noticed, she said nothing; and his father, looking his way now, also said nothing. So Isaac took a sip. It was bitter despite the sugar and milk, and terribly strong, as he'd always imagined it would be. But somehow the adults had liked it. They were laughing harder than ever now, probably at the face he was making. Charlotte and Erwin had drunk theirs without even wincing. Maybe they were used to it, maybe he wasn't. He took another sip to accustom himself.

That night Erwin showed Isaac how to load his Christmas camera with color film, but when it was done and Isaac put his eye to the viewfinder, Erwin turned his face away. Isaac understood; there was no need for his father's warning, the raised eyebrow. Charlotte wore a blue dress that night.

Holy Toledo

Looking for the charm against the Evil Eye, Nadia stretched up on the footstool – a tomboy in her dungarees – and searched the shelves of the bathroom cabinet one by one. The charm was a tiny object, no larger than a rosary bead, and it was forever getting lost. But despite the clutter of this house (her grandmother threw nothing away) it was forever turning up again, too.

Sitti, her grandmother, had had the amulet ever since the old country when she herself was a child. A Lazerine monk claimed he'd found it lying amid the rubble of an ancient excavation and, hoping to gain some favor, he brought it directly to Sitti's uncle, the district magistrate. When the monk was gone – the favor granted or not, Sitti never said – her uncle simply looked down at the charm in his hand and shrugged. After all, what was this thing to him? Nothing more than a drop of porcelain painted to look like a miniature eyeball. And so the amulet was forgotten, mislaid until after his death when it turned up again among his things. No one claimed it, so Sitti decided to keep the charm for herself. Attaching it to a stiff golden thread, she'd had the amulet ever since, over the years misplacing it, yet always finding it again somewhere.

But not here. Here on the top shelf there were only razors, old women's salves, and jars of black ointments

meant to be kept out of a child's reach. Nadia stepped down from the footstool and carried it back into the front room.

"Achhh. . . ."

The long, familiar moan floated down the hallway from the kitchen; Sitti must be searching there now. And Mikhail was still in the front room where Nadia had left him, still doing nothing to help.

"Mikhi," she said, "it wasn't in the bathroom either."

"It doesn't matter," he said. Crossing his legs on the sofa, her brother spoke without turning to look at her.

"Then it has to be in the cellar. Me and Sitti, we looked everyplace else." Mikhail said nothing. "I bet I know where in the cellar, too." She waited for him to ask where. He didn't. "How much you want to bet," she went on anyway, "that it's in one of those boxes Uncle Eddie took down there last spring?"

Still her brother said nothing. He would not even look at her.

"Mikhi? You wouldn't just sit there if Uncle Eddie was here. He'll give you the belt again for not helping."

At that, Mikhi turned his gaze, slowly, the wide brown eyes of their father. "You telling?"

"No, not *me*." She wanted very much for him to believe this, but even as she spoke she realized that her voice was too solemn, unnatural in its earnestness. "I meant *Sitti*."

"Don't make me laugh." He was her little brother by two years, yet it seemed always as if he were the older one. Nadia was the one who giggled and could keep no secrets.

With another loud moan, Sitti left the kitchen and went into the dining room directly next to them. They remained motionless, silent in the ticking stillness of the front room lest she hear them and be reminded of their presence in her house: maybe if she forgot that someone

was here to listen she would stop groaning that way—achh—every time she bent over, every time she pulled open a drawer or leaned back her head against the dizziness.

"Achhh. . . ."

(It hadn't been long after breakfast—maybe she was still drinking her coffee—when the pain and the groaning began. "What's wrong, Sitti?" Mikhi kept asking her over and over, but she wouldn't answer. Later, as the noon heat grew unbearable to her, she undressed, put on a nightgown, and braided her hair up off her neck.)

Sitti was a short woman, her broad hips spreading the nightgown as she bent low to pull and shove at the buffet drawers. Nadia almost smiled, watching her through the archway; the nightgown was white, and except for the three iron braids sticking out, her grandmother looked from behind like a little fat altar boy.

"Achhh. . . ."

Her groans were getting louder, and a hint of worry flickered across Mikhi's eyes. Then, just as quickly, he brightened, curling himself into a hollow of the sofa and tucking the souvenir cushions one under each arm so that their tasseled corners met beneath his chin like a silver beard. He grunted twice, as if to hold his sister's attention, then he made a face at her—an old man wagging a toothless mouth—and she had to turn away to keep from laughing out loud.

"Achhh. . . ." It was Arabic, but Nadia knew it meant nothing, wasn't even a word so much as the sound of effort and pain.

The drawers were crammed full of all sorts of odds and ends, and Sitti would be busy there a long time. That was her way: looking for one thing, she had to stop and muse over every other thing she came across. She could throw nothing away.

The satin pillows looked smooth and cool against

84

Mikhi's hands. The American pillows, Sitti called them. Uncle Eddie had brought them home for her from the navy. The blue one had on its decorated side the figures of anchors and stars, the red one a poem stitched in silver thread. When he came home to stay, Uncle Eddie read the poem aloud to Sitti, showing her how the first letter of each line spelled the word *Mother*. The women said that Sitti was lucky to have at least one son who cared so much for his mother. What they meant, of course, was that the children's father did not care so much because he left. Especially since Papa was the elder son and it was his duty to stay. More than that, the custom still held, even here in America: a widower with children is expected to either remarry or else return to his mother's house. Papa did neither. Instead, he remained in his own house after the funeral. For almost five years until, one hot July morning, he dressed Mikhi and Nadia in their Sunday clothes and brought them to Sitti's house, all their things packed in grocery bags. And after that he simply went away.

Nadia watched a moment more as her brother's fingers brushed lightly over the stitching, tracing stars and letters, then she stood up. "I'm going to look in Sitti's room again."

Mikhi looked up from the cushions. The charm wasn't in Sitti's room, they both knew that; the bedrooms had been searched twice already, and all she was doing now was simply trying to put off having to go down to the cellar alone. Mikhi's wry, sidelong glance mocked her.

She crossed in front of him, ignoring the face he once more made at her, lipping his teeth that way to get her laughing. She was only eleven, and a girl given to giggling, but she wasn't a fool. Mikhi was up to something, all day just sitting there and doing nothing to help. There was going to be trouble—once more Uncle Eddie would have his snakeskin belt out and flashing—and she

would be a part of it. She'd have to be. Mikhi was younger than her, yet she had always followed his lead, even into trouble.

"Mikhi?" she paused in the doorway. "I don't want to go down there alone." Nadia kept her eyes downward on a curled edge of the rug. Sitti was dying, or said she was, and she needed the amulet to ease the pain of her dying. At least it might quiet her. "Will you come with me when I go?"

Again he didn't answer. Nadia stomped angrily into the hall—her dungarees, bought large so she'd grow into them, slap-slapping at her ankles—and pushed open the bedroom door.

Sitti's room was papered with dark flowers. The walls, like everything else in that house, were cluttered. Holy pictures hung in uneven diamond patterns above the bed, and there were photographs everywhere, dark-framed pictures of Sitti when she was young, of Jiddo—Nadia's grandfather—rimmed in black because he was dead, and of Papa and Uncle Eddie when they were little boys. None of them were smiling, not even little Papa, his big eyes staring blankly at her through the dusty glass.

The dresser top had been cleared at least twice that day, and there was nothing on it now but a small statue of the Virgin. Almost two years before, when Uncle Eddie was still in the navy and it looked like he might be sent to Korea, Sitti had taped a folded dollar bill to the statue's base. Like a prayer, almost.

(". . . Great to be back," Uncle Eddie had kept saying after his discharge. "Great to be back."

"What was it like?" visitors would ask.

"We never did go overseas, unless you count once to Panama. Mostly it was up and down the West Coast."

"And how was that?"

"Truth is, I was lost the whole time. Really. I never knew where I was. And when we put in it was even

worse. I was always getting lost in the cities. You honestly don't know what homesick is until you've been out there."

Then Uncle Eddie would take his mother's hand in both of his. "Great to be back." He praised her cooking every single day of that first week home. "Great to be back," he said it even to himself, idly fingering one of the sofa doilies, then actually noticing it, as if discovering at his very fingertips yet one more familiar marker against the lostness from which he had returned. . . .)

The bedroom was warm, musty with the smell of sleep. Nadia opened a window, then knelt and put her face to the faint breeze. Except for the furniture and the pictures, this could have been her old bedroom at home. The two houses were almost identical, both built of glazed brick with tall, narrow windows and rooms that were dark even in daytime since they shared walls with the rowhouses on either side (and beneath those rooms the cellars, damp honeycombs of thick walls and uneven floors); both houses, too, were within that same general neighborhood of East Detroit, the Little Syria centered at Congress Street and Larned. Pressing her face to the window screen, she could see the dome of the Maronite Catholic Church and the onion shaped twin steeples of the Greek Orthodox. Farther up Congress there were shops that sold woven artifacts and brass from the old country. They had food, too, things that couldn't be found anywhere else in Detroit; pressed apricots, goat cheese, sesame paste and pine nuts and briny olives. ("The food, that's what I missed most," Uncle Eddie said. "The Americans, they don't know how to eat.") And there were the *ahwa* shops too, where old men sat all day amid tobacco smoke and the bitter smell of Turkish coffee.

On Saturday mornings Americans came into the neighborhood to shop. Women, mostly, the merchants called them "Mum" (and behind their backs "College

Mum," not so much because of the university nearby as for the way these women spoke English—everything in the nose). Nadia often used to sit outside just to watch the college mums pass. While most women dressed up in hat and gloves to go shopping, clutching a narrow black purse, the college mums seemed younger than that. They always had on something bright, like a scarf or a bandanna. The handbags slung carelessly from their shoulders were huge, made of woven rope or straw, and patterned with beads. Usually they wore no makeup, and with their hair pinned up or back there was always something boyish about their faces. A few even dressed in trousers, like men. And they were always excited about something, always smiling as they pointed out this or that to a companion who'd never been there before, exclaiming too loudly about the inlay work on a cedar music box or the smell of a foreign spice, and always asking "Oh, and what do you call *this?*" as if they'd never seen a barrel of olives before. The shopkeepers would smile back at them and say *olives* in Arabic, and the college mums loved that, chattering on and on as they spent their money. By early afternoon they would begin leaving—silly women—and always Nadia wished that she were one of them, returning with them into that huge strangeness, America, luring her despite the threat it seemed to hold of loss and vicious homesickness.

*

"Achhh. . . ."

The drawers of Sitti's dresser were sticking with the heat, and Nadia had to tug hard to open them. In a corner of the bottom drawer, tucked beneath the stockings and yellowed underwear, were several envelopes banded together. These contained photographs never pasted into the album books, among them the two or three remaining pictures of Nadia's mother. Since she was an American, the old people hardly ever mentioned her

when they talked of the dead. Nadia barely remembered her at all, and she always envied Mikhi who, though younger, could state with the quiet assurance of a witness that their mother's eyes, which were so dark in the photographs, had been bright blue.

Cached also amid the underthings were broken rosaries, pages from Arabic prayerbooks, shreds of holy palms plaited years ago into the shapes of crosses and crowns of thorns. Although the younger people gave such things a kind of grudging respect (the whole time he was at sea Uncle Eddie wore the charm against the Evil Eye – the very one that was missing now – and he said he wasn't the only one on his ship with a lucky piece), it was usually just the old people who were careful not to point at certain stars, who never ate from a yellow dish or left a slipper upside down with its sole stepping on God's face. Once, Nadia told her uncle about how Mikhi had imitated the ritual that old people had of kissing a piece of bread that had fallen to the floor. It was so funny, she had to tell somebody; Mikhi popping his eyes in exaggerated horror as the bread fell, the reverence with which he picked it up and kissed it, finally working his mouth sideways and sucking passionately, the way people kissed in movies.

Uncle Eddie didn't laugh. Instead, he simply lit a cigarette. Nadia began to worry as she watched the smoke puff twice with each rapid double-drag. It was a busy, nervous way of smoking that Uncle Eddie had learned in the navy. Her uncle had always been quick to laugh at almost anything. But as the months passed after his return from the service, Eddie seemed to grow more serious, more easily irritated. Some said that it had started while he was still in the navy, just after he'd heard that Papa was gone.

The cigarette was still lit when Mikhi came in from playing outside. Uncle Eddie drew one last double-drag and tapped it out in a saucer. Then he removed his belt

and called Mikhi into the kitchen. Nadia hadn't meant to tattle. She tried to show Mikhi this by the look on her face, but Mikhi saw only the belt as he backed slowly away from the kitchen door.

The narrow snakeskin belt was one of the first things that Eddie had bought after the service. He was in San Diego and not yet out of uniform when he passed a shop window, and the gleam of its scales caught his eye.

"Achhh. . . ."

The moans were growing louder, and from the front room Nadia heard a sound like something thrown against the wall, something soft. She pushed the last drawer shut and went out to see.

The front door stood wide open, the screen door ajar. And Mikhi was gone. The cushion he'd thrown, the red one, lay across the room, wedged between the baseboard and an end table.

Nervous, like Papa, he never could bear it the way she could. ("She's old, Mikhi," she used to tell him. "Old people get sick, then they die. That's all.") And so to find the amulet, she would have to go down alone into the cellar. He had left that to her.

She lingered a moment, listening while the groans became soft again, as regular as the tiny pendulum swings of the mantel clock. Nadia was afraid to go down there alone, and Mikhi knew it, and here he'd gone off anyway and left it to her.

She ran the fingers of one hand through her hair, an absent gesture; then, suddenly aware of the gesture, she dropped her hand to her side. Another moment of that and the tears would have started for sure.

*

Her father had a way of combing his fingers through his hair when he was worried, the nervous habit of a nervous man. His gray hair stood out in whorls because of it. And on that day almost three years ago (even into adulthood she and her brother would remark the very

date their father brought them to Sitti's house and left them there: Sunday, July the eighth, 1951) it seemed that every few seconds his hand would go up to his hair as they waited on the front stoop for Sitti to answer her door. They waited a long time, and when she did answer, how grim she was, how stone-faced, as she let them in. The bags they carried were heavy, even though Nadia herself had repacked them. (Papa had packed them first, confused from the start, unsure of what to take and what to throw out or leave behind.) He never came in after them but remained on the stoop as if still confused. There was a frightened sadness in the way he stood there, and his kiss was a good-bye.

Afterward, nobody spoke much of him except to repeat what was already known: that Mikhail Yakoub — married late in life (and to an American), a failure at any business he tried, finally a widower with children — was never a lucky man.

But then Mikhail Yakoub never respected luck as the others did, not even grudgingly. He preferred to be free of it. "Bad luck or good luck," Nadia remembered him saying, "to hell with them both." One time, he took her and Mikhi with him on an errand down Congress Street. While there, he stopped in at one of the *ahwa* shops to talk to a man. The coffee shops did not admit females, not even little girls; she had to wait at the door while her father and brother went inside. The windows, like the doorway, were wide open, and flies buzzed everywhere among the tables. Old men sat drinking from tiny cups, all of them smoking cigars or water pipes. A group at a near table were playing cards. Suddenly, one of these men looked up as a shadow flitted past the lamp shade dangling above him. Then they were all scrambling to their feet, crying out and cursing. A chair was overturned, and Nadia had to step aside to keep from getting trampled as the men jostled and elbowed one another out the door and onto the street. She heard her father

before she saw him, his loud laugh booming above the confusion. Only after the three of them had woven their way through the small crowd did Mikhi, himself red-faced with laughter, pause long enough to explain it to her.

"What happened is, is a bird flew in the window."

"So?" she said.

"It's an omen," her father said.

"A bad one?"

"The worst. It means a death in the house. Holy Toledo," her father began laughing again, "I never saw a room clear out so fast."

Nadia chuckled a little, even though she didn't see anything funny, not at first. Holy Toledo was a city near Detroit, and Papa called out its name sometimes when things were funny. But after a moment, remembering how quickly the old men had moved, their baggy trousers flapping as they shuffled and pushed, she began to laugh in earnest.

"I almost hurt myself," Papa was saying, and the children hurried after him to hear, "when old Stamos the Greek tried to climb out a window. I had to grab him by the suspenders and hold him back."

And so her father never respected luck, himself luckless. After he went away, those people who mentioned Mikhail Yakoub at all spoke of him as if he were gone forever. But he wasn't dead – she and Mikhi had been able to wheedle that much out of them. He had simply disappeared from the neighborhood. And when the children pressed to know where he'd gone, some said "Boston," others "Chicago," but none of them was certain. Sitti answered them only by saying "America!" and fluttering fingers to temple in the Arabic gesture *tarit*, which meant *it has flown out*. Yet how could that which was sealed within the hard bone of the skull simply fly away? Nadia couldn't understand it, and so she clung to what

was certain: he was gone, swallowed up somehow by the vast America beyond these streets, alive, forever luckless, and free. And in her imagination forever homesick, too, forever standing at a closed door somewhere, lost, running his fingers through his hair.

*

Still blinking against the tears—not much of a tomboy after all—she was startled to find the cellar stairs already lit. "Mikhi?" she called.

The stairwell before her was cool despite the day's heat, its walls seeping spiderwebs of black moisture.

"Mikhi?"

"Down here, Nadia. Come on down here." Her brother's voice was clapped instantly from behind by a thin, sharp echo.

"Did you find it?" she asked, leaning into the doorway. It was quiet for a moment, then she heard his voice again, thinned so by the echo that she thought of the sound of her own voice, as if from far away.

"Okay, Nadia?"

"Okay what?"

"Are you coming down?"

"Is it there? Did you look in the boxes?"

"Aww, Nadia!" The way he called her name, thin and sad from within that darkness, it was a plea. She hesitated, then descended quickly after it, the way medicine is swallowed quickly so as not to taste it.

"Where are you?" she called. The cellar gradually deepened into its maze of half-walls that baffled, then blocked altogether the faint stairwell light.

"In here."

She stepped cautiously along the uneven floor, following her brother's voice into a corner room. The only light was a smudged glow from the single high window. Mikhi sat beneath the window, legs dangling atop Sitti's old steamer trunk.

"Did you find it?"

"I didn't look." Mikhi's voice caught. "Aww, Nadia. It doesn't matter."

"But why didn't you just—" she stopped herself, realizing that Mikhi probably had come down here for her sake, because she was afraid and she'd asked him to come with her. And the strange thing was that she wasn't so scared anymore. At least not now. There she was in the deepest corner of the cellar; she almost laughed.

When she turned to Mikhi, his head was down, eyes on the trunk beneath him. Brass and black leather, one side of the trunk was crayoned with writing from forty years ago. Their father had once pointed out to them the different languages—Turkish, Arabic, French, and finally, in English, the yellow and blue admittance stamp of Ellis Island, New York.

"What is it, Mikhi? What's wrong?"

"She's not going to die," he said with sureness. Then, the sureness faltering: "Do you think she's going to die?"

"Yes."

"Honest?"

"She's old, Mikhi. Old people—"

"I don't care," he said quickly. "I'm going anyway."

"Where?"

For a moment there was silence—only the muffled sounds of Sitti's footsteps above them—before Mikhi sighed, "I don't know...out there. Away from here." Then he touched his hair with his fingertips.

"Don't do that," Nadia said, and he lowered his hand. "When are you going?"

"I don't know."

She nodded once, slowly, as if in solemn agreement, but it was relief that she felt. If he didn't know where and he didn't know when, then maybe he wouldn't really go. And then she wouldn't have to go either, be-

cause what would they do? Who would take care of them out there in America, a girl and her little brother?

"I mean it, Nadia."

But he didn't mean it, not really. Alone, Mikhi wouldn't know what to do. Not even what to take and what to leave behind. Especially that. He wouldn't know that any more than Papa had known it.

"Nadia, will you come with me?"

"Sure," she answered quickly, easily. After all, a boy can't just walk off the way a man does.

"It doesn't matter," Mikhi said, the disappointment in his voice showing her that she'd answered too quickly. "But at least you won't tell on me, will you?"

"I don't tattle. Not anymore."

Above them, Sitti was moving something heavy, dragging it across the floor. Her moans carried even to the cellar.

"You promise?"

He still didn't believe her. She began to promise, but just then the moans from upstairs were cut short by a brief cry of surprise as something, glass or china, shattered on the dining room floor. The two of them remained still for a moment of teetering imbalance that ended abruptly with a heavy, resounding thump. Mikhi leaped from the trunk and ran ahead of her up the stairs.

"Help to stand," Sitti said, hearing the sound of their feet. She had fallen to her knees, the side of her face leaning against an open drawer of the buffet. She must have been trying to shove the buffet away from the wall so she could search behind it.

"Sitti," Mikhi spoke quickly, "should I go find Uncle Eddie?"

"No," Sitti said, whispering, as if she had strength only for that. "Jus' help to stand." She held out one arm, and Mikhi took it.

"Ach!" she cried out at the force of his grip. Immediately, Mikhi released the hand.

"My heart," Sitti hugged herself, "my heart. Achhh. . . ."

"Is it a heart attack?" Mikhi's voice rose on the word *attack*, threatening to rise to a screech if she answered yes, but Sitti didn't answer. Instead, she braced her forearms against the buffet and slowly, but with less effort than Nadia had imagined it would take, raised herself to her feet.

"Did you find it, Sitti?" Nadia asked. She looked down at the shattered remains of what had been the china teapot. "Was it in the tea—"

Sitti closed her eyes as if to silence her. She stood that way for a few seconds, consulting some inner pain. Then the three braids that stuck out over the collar of her nightgown quivered a little, and she belched, a low weak sound.

"G'wan," she told them—they were staring at her—"G'wan, don't lookit me." She leaned against the buffet. "Achhh. . . ."

"What *is* it, Sitti?" Again Mikhi's voice rose, like a girl's.

"Nothing. G'wan."

"Can I get you something? What do you want us to *do?*"

"Nothing," she answered, but simply, even lightly, as if somehow pleased.

Mikhi looked to Nadia. His eyes were wide, near panic. Then he lowered his head and spoke. "You're not sick," he said.

There was utter silence, and Nadia was frightened by the sudden realization that she was about to laugh.

"You're not sick at all," Mikhi said once more, looking up now. He was actually smiling, although his eyes kept blinking as if somebody were shaking a fist in front of them. "You're all right. It's just gas. I know it is."

"You be shaddap!" Sitti growled. Then she cursed him in Arabic, "*Ibn menyouk!*"

Mikhi flinched, but stood firm. "You're not sick," he said again.

Sitti turned furiously to Nadia, as to a witness. Mikhi, too was looking at her now. Then, slowly, he shifted his gaze to Sitti, and her face collapsed in fear at the sight of him. She raised both hands to her eyes and began to cry out weakly, muttering like a child on the verge of tears.

*

"And that was when he give to me the Evil Eye, *ya djinn, ya ibn menyouk!* The girl here, she see it all!"

Uncle Eddie listened patiently while Sitti went on and on, slipping in and out of Arabic and rushing the words so rapidly together that the children—made to sit quietly at the kitchen table—could barely follow it. She paced back and forth behind Mikhi's chair, and Nadia watched her uncle smoke his cigarette with those nervous double-drags. Now and then, distractedly, he reached to his neck and touched the golden thread. The charm against the Evil Eye was suspended from it, a single porcelain gleam at the hair of his throat. Nadia had noticed it as soon as he walked in the house. She was sure Mikhi must have seen it. And Sitti too, as she hurried to the door, grasping Eddie's sleeve with both hands before he was hardly inside. Uncle Eddie didn't even try to hide it. All he did was shrug—a son cowed by the suddenness of his mother's fury—and call her and Mikhi into the kitchen. Then Sitti started all over again from the beginning: Mikhi had been tormenting her all day. Worse yet, she was sick to dying, and the boy gave her the Evil Eye—wasn't that so, Nadia?

She squirmed in her chair, answering neither yes nor no. She was innocent, but for the first time uneasy in the tattletale pleasure of such innocence; after all, Mikhi

was right. Here their grandmother stood, alive, hands working as she spoke, and her voice strong. She wasn't sick at all. Mikhi knew that. She wasn't going to die.

"Isn't that so, Nadia? Speak up, girl," Sitti paused only a second before again launching into an angry jabber of Arabic.

And the charm, all the good luck of it hanging there at Eddie's throat the whole time they were searching, seemed forgotten; its luck granted or not – both Sitti and Uncle Eddie were acting now as if it never mattered in the first place. And Mikhi had known that too.

Her brother was watching her. She could feel the heat of his stare, and she turned to him. *No matter what you answer,* his look told her, *I'm still going to catch it.* Then he turned away. *So save yourself,* his turning away said, and she was free.

"Well, Nadia?"

Uncle Eddie put out his cigarette. Then he reached down and rested one hand on the buckle of the snakeskin belt, waiting.

"Sitti isn't sick," she found herself saying, and so calmly that her own voice sounded strange to her. "And all Mikhi did, he just looked at her, that's all. It wasn't the Evil Eye."

"Ach!" Sitti was furious, betrayed.

And so, after Mikhi got the belt, Nadia would be next. She knew that. But already, calmly, she was beginning to think about what it would be like for them afterward. It would not be easy; even so, she felt a wordless yet certain anticipation: the two of them luckless, free in Boston and Chicago and Holy Toledo, the rest of their lives lost in the American homesickness. What should they take with them?

Next to her, Mikhi released a nervous sound, almost a laugh.

Then it was over, her brother's voice cut off in the

suck of breath as Uncle Eddie reached out to grasp him by the arm. The belt flashed, and Mikhi shrieked with each sharp flick and slap, again and again and again.

Nadia would be next. Calmly, she closed her eyes and tried to imagine America, how it will be, and what they should take with them when they go.

And What Else?

Only an hour or so after sunrise it begins getting hot on the street. But it is still quiet, and the faint honk and roar of the traffic farther downtown only adds to the silence and the sense of hush. A boy, who will one day marry an American girl and open his own supermarket with her family's money, begins sweeping with wide, playful strokes in front of the grocery store. Slanted morning light fills Monroe Street with yellow, pushing the shadows of lamp posts and fire hydrants and boy down the long concrete. Scattered by the broom, wine bottles and beer bottles glisten as they roll along the curb to the gutter. The red brick of the buildings warms in the sun, the old, silent buildings that will be torn down twenty years from now, in the summer of 1958, and the holes they leave paved over.

Across the street a man turns the corner, a fishing rod and canvas sack in his hands. He is staring up as he turns, his eyes on the rooftops, and because of the silence of the morning, the slap-slap of his large shoes (he wears no stockings) carries all the way to where the boy has stopped sweeping to watch, shielding the sun from his eyes with what looks like a half-hearted salute. A woman, curled asleep in a doorway, stretches out her legs. The boy shouts a warning, but the man does not look down. He walks directly into the feet and stumbles

forward on his hands and knees. He falls slowly, and it seems to the boy that with a little more balancing, a little more waving of the arms back and forth and trembling of the knees, he might not have fallen at all.

The man picks up the rod and sack and, saying nothing, nudges the woman several times in the legs with his toe. She stirs and rolls over, still asleep. The man moves on. When he has crossed the street, the boy puts a finger to his lips and points to the roof of the apartment above the store. A pair of pigeons flutters timid on the spine of a gabled window. The man sees. He smiles his thanks to the boy, then clicks the safety of his reel, and the heavy lead sinker, followed by a dozen hooks, falls and dangles about a foot from the tip of the rod. The boy salutes with both hands as he looks up again. One of the pigeons looks down from its perch, and the man casts. The heavy lead strikes, the hooks catch and dig. Blue-gray feathers fall in a small, thick cloud and the man and boy shout, filling the street with their noise.

"Got three of 'em for ya," the man says, and he dumps the sack on the thick wooden block in back of the store. "One of 'em's still alive."

The butcher, whose English is not so good, puts down his knife and takes the living pigeon out of the sack. "Habeeb," he says to the boy, his son, "get for this bum three bottlesa beer." The man smiles, grateful, and the butcher returns the smile as he twists the neck of the living pigeon. "An' I make you san'wich, too," he says.

Since there is a bar on either side of the grocery store, and three more across the street, and since, moreover, the store itself sells beer and wine to carry out, the word "bum" is the first English the boy and his father have learned. They use it as Uncle E, the owner of the store, uses it, brother to the boy's grandfather, who refers to neighborhood adults (those neither Syrian nor Lebanese) as bums, and who, on this summer morning, lies silent in his bed in the apartment upstairs, awake

and thinking about—only God knows, for Uncle E has spoken to no one for nearly a year.

But when Uncle E ran the store, when his wife Maheeba was still living and the boy and his father were new to this country, he would stand behind his butcher block and shout to the boy's father, "Ya Milad! This bum, he's gonna sweep out the backa the store!" And Milad, the boy's father, would show the man the back room and a broom. Then the boy, a preschooler in those days, would be told to sit in the back (with a bottle of soda pop) and yell like hell if the man tried to run off with anything. But the bums never tried to run off with anything, not once in the boy's memory. When the job was finished Uncle E would cut the man a thick slice of liverwurst and open him a bottle of beer. And even if the man had not only done a good job (getting the sawdust out of the cracks in the floor), but was stone sober as well, Uncle E still called him a bum. He checked the back room and looked at the boy's father. "This bum, he did a good job." He had no other word. "You come back," he told the man, if the job was well done. The man would nod. Bums hardly said anything, and when they did their voices were high pitched, asking for one more of something, a sandwich or a beer. But they never got it. Once Aunt Maheeba gave the boy a candy bar and sent him running after a bum, a very lean man, who had asked for another sandwich. He took it from the boy without a word, unwrapped it, and ate it as he walked away.

The next English the boy had picked up was "enwaddyelse." Uncle E said this when he completed an order for a customer. After weighing and wrapping a cut of meat, he placed the package on the counter, smiled at the customer, and asked in a pleasant voice, "Enwaddyelse?" And what else? Aunt Maheeba, too, said this after ringing an order through on the cash register. A regular customer said, "Nothing, thank you," or

"That's all for now, thanks," but new customers did not understand at first. "Huh?" they said, or "Whazzat again?" So Aunt Maheeba would say it again, slowly and distinctly, just as she had learned it from Uncle E, "En-waddy-else?" If they still did not understand, she smiled her terribly charming smile that Uncle E talked so much about before his silence and handed over the change. "Tank-you verry much," she said, and this they understood.

But "enwaddyelse" was not used only with customers. Uncle E used it when his patience with Maheeba ran out. This usually happened when a customer came in with a large order. At such times the boy and his father roamed the small area of the store, finding the articles the customer asked for and bringing them to the counter. There, Uncle E would wipe his hands across the large stomach of his apron and begin wrapping with brown paper and string. As he did so, he read the price, which was marked in English, translated, and called it out in Arabic to his wife, who translated the Arabic to French and found the numbers on the cash register. At times, usually when she was suffering from one of her headaches, Aunt Maheeba would begin to cry as she muttered the numbers in French. After a little while she would sit on the small stool behind the counter and press an apron to her face. When this happened Uncle E knew that the last three or four prices he had called were not rung correctly. "Enwaddyelse!" he would shout, and take over the cash register. Then Aunt Maheeba would move to the end of the counter and wrap, reading the numbers in French, calling them out in Arabic. The work went slow, then, for Aunt Maheeba was not quick at wrapping, and Uncle E, who found it difficult translating Arabic numbers to English, took his time.

With the boy, too, he often lost his patience. When the boy begged his uncle for a nickel (he was a softer touch than Milad, and Aunt Maheeba never had any

money) the old man would at first refuse with a click of his tongue. Then as the boy insisted, anxious to buy a roll of caps for his toy pistol, Uncle E would say in Arabic, "Stop! Enough!" So the boy would sit at the bottom of the stairs that led up to the apartment, curl his lips, and sulk. After a few minutes of silence Uncle E would look up from the leg of lamb he was slicing. The boy, too, would look up, and their eyes would meet, look away, meet again, and Uncle E would wipe his hands, reach into his pocket, and slap a nickel on the butcher block. "Enwaddyelse?" And what else? The boy would grab the nickel and kiss his uncle's hand. "Truly," he answered in Arabic, "there is nothing else."

*

Milad soaks the pigeons in the sink behind the butcher block. Behind him, sitting on a wooden fold-out chair, the man who had caught the pigeons is finishing his second beer.

"This is a fine boy ya got here," he says to Milad, putting his hand on the boy's head and pressing down lightly.

Milad does not turn around. "Leave da kid alone," he says. He looks at the Coca-Cola clock above the sink. "G'wan, get Uncle E his oatmeal."

The boy ducks away from under the man's hand and runs upstairs to the kitchen. As he lights the stove with a match, he can hear Uncle E moving around in the bathroom on the other side of the wall. The oatmeal cooks, and the boy, who can only wait, stands on a chair and looks out the window at the flat tar roof and the pigeons that walk on it. The sun is higher now, and its heat rises from the black surface of the roof, making everything shimmer before the boy's eyes. He steps down and gets a bowl and spoon ready. Uncle E still has not come out. This makes the boy uneasy for he once found his uncle passed out and bloody on the toilet. Turning the fire off under the oatmeal, he knocks on the bathroom door.

Uncle E opens almost immediately, smiles quickly, and shuts the door again. The boy cups his hands to the keyhole and says that the oatmeal is ready. Uncle E says nothing. He has said nothing for nearly a year.

"Doctor Binatti says it is goddamn stubbornness," Milad tells the different guests who visit after mass every Sunday. "He even called specialists and they could find nothing wrong with his voice."

"The poor man is past seventy," one of the guests would always say.

"And strong as a mule," Milad says to this.

"He has had an operation, and still his stomach pains him."

"And still he sneaks his whiskey."

"It is for the pain," the guest would say. "He has lived to see the death of his children, and now his wife too, God give her rest."

"God give her rest, she has been dead more than a year. Grief should not last this long."

"She was young."

"Doctor Binatti was right."

"Not even fifty."

"Goddamn stubbornness."

Aunt Maheeba, though never really a robust person, had seemed healthy enough just the same. Yet she died one night in the middle of her sleep. Uncle E had called up the stairwell to her, yelling for his breakfast, shouting that customers were coming in already. Finally he sent Milad upstairs to find out why she did not answer. And when Milad had come back down his face was yellow. "Get Doctor Binatti, quickly, quickly," he told his son in Arabic. So the boy ran up Monroe Street to the doctor's office above the barber shop, and Doctor Binatti took his black bag from a shelf behind the desk, shouted at the nurse who had just taken her coat off, and hurried after the boy. (In later years the boy would go to Doctor Binatti's office in the twelfth storey of the downtown

medical building. The doctor would hug the boy and in his huge and booming voice he would say, so that all the waiting room could hear, "Habeeb, Habeeb, when you came to this country you were fulla worms and I had to clean you out!" Then he would kiss the boy on his forehead and ask what was the matter. The boy would say, very quietly, "The flu," or "My nose is plugged up again." Doctor Binatti died in 1954 of a heart attack. At the time he was chief surgeon for Mercy Hospital, and he died at the hospital, in an elevator.)

Aunt Maheeba was in bed. She had died there in the night, and Uncle E thought she was still sleeping when he got up to open the store. Doctor Binatti said he wasn't sure, but he thought it was a blood clot. Then Uncle E, who had been quiet and shaking all this time, spat on the floor and at the top of his voice he goddamned blood clots; he goddamned Doctor Binatti; he goddamned the boy and his father and himself; and he went downstairs to close the store, goddamning the customers as he chased them out.

The Maronite priest from Cleveland came and said a Syrian funeral. Afterward, at the cemetery, Uncle E picked a white carnation from a wreath that was placed near him and dropped it into the open grave. Then he opened his mouth (he wept like a child, with his mouth open) and began the wail, "Ya Maheeba, ya Maheeba," and his voice broke the hearts of all the mourners. So they joined him in the lament until the tears choked off their own voices and they stood dumb, dropping flowers into the hole. The boy, too, picked a carnation and, stepping up close to the lip of the grave, threw the flower in. He swung his whole arm into it, and the flower shot down and struck the casket lid with a hollow knock. The sound was loud, seemed to come from within the box, and the boy ran to find his father's knees.

"It is a hard thing," Uncle E used to say after that.

He would be standing over the butcher block, slicing a thick liver with smooth strokes or flipping a carcass to where he could cut the meat from the bone. The customer would stand on the other side of the scale and answer him in Arabic.

"It is God's will, bless His name."

"Bless His name," Uncle E would say, using the standard response. But after a pause he'd add, "She should not have been the first."

"Elias," the customer would say to this, "there is nothing to be done. God give her rest, she is with the saints."

"I am past seventy," he'd say, "I should be with the saints," and he'd wipe his hands on the already bloody apron. "Not Maheeba."

"Elias, if you talk too much about her, God give her rest, you will make yourself sick." And Milad, standing behind the cash register, would agree. "There is nothing more to say, Uncle."

Then Uncle E would wrap the customer's order and ask if there was anything else. "That's all," the customer would say. "Just don't make yourself sick."

But Uncle E had made himself sick. His stomach hurt him, and he refused to eat Milad's cooking. Instead he fixed his own meals, sandwiches of raw lamb meat ground with onions and cracked wheat. In the evenings he sat in the alley in back of the store with two or three bums. The boy joined them sometimes, hidden in the darkness, until a glance from his uncle sent him back into the store. The old man, older in the light of the small bulb above the back door, drank whiskey then, for the pain, and he talked about the store, Roosevelt, the old country, but never about Maheeba, not to the bums. They sat or squatted over the stones of the alley, listening to him, drinking from the bottle as it came around. When the bottle returned to Uncle E, he wiped its mouth with the palm of his hand.

Finally, because the raw meat did not heal his stomach, and the whiskey did less and less for the pain, Uncle E saw Doctor Binatti.

"Elias, what's the trouble?" The doctor's giant voice echoed into the waiting room where the boy sat between two women, paging through a comic book he could not read.

"The pain, Doctor. I got pain."

"Elias, you were born with pain, you live with pain, you're gonna die with pain! Take off your shirt."

"Enwaddyelse?" This was angry, and the boy looked up toward the closed door. But a moment later one of them mumbled something, and the laughter of both their big voices shook the office. A woman in a corner chair smiled at the boy. He turned sideways on the couch and stared straight at the comic, his face in a pretended scowl. He knew he was cute and that American ladies were not used to seeing such curls. With a little twist of his head he made a face in her direction. She chuckled and looked away, smiling at the far wall.

For several weeks Uncle E took the milky white medicine that Doctor Binatti had prescribed, ate only the foods listed on a paper the nurse had given him, and, for a while, even stopped drinking whiskey. But still he talked.

"It is a hard thing," he would say to the boy's father, and to customers in the store, and to relatives when they came to visit on Sundays. "It is a hard thing," and he would nod his head; and the listeners would nod their heads and say nothing.

"Why is it you say nothing?"

"Elias, is there anything else to say? God give her rest, she is with the saints."

"The saints!" He spat on the floor. "Goddamn every one of them! Listen to this. . . ." And Uncle E would tell another of his stories about Aunt Maheeba, about how she was a child when he met her in the old country and

she could already read and write French, or about the courage she showed at the funerals of both their sons, how she got him to go to Mass several times, even how it was to go upstairs after opening the store and find her sitting at the kitchen table with her black hair undone, brushed down her back, and breakfast smelling just ready.

The boy sat with the others and listened. When the story was finished, he, too, was silent.

*

In September before he started school, the boy had found Uncle E on the floor of the bathroom. The toilet was full of blood, and he began to scream down the stairwell to his father. His father ran up the stairs, and one of the customers called an ambulance.

At Mercy Hospital, Doctor Binatti came out of the emergency room and told Milad to send after a priest. The boy began to cry when he heard this, and the doctor picked him up and carried him into the elevator. He tickled the boy on the way up and left him in the lobby with a comic book from the gift shop.

The boy waited and, as time passed, grew hungry. The clock on the wall was no help, for the movement of its hands meant nothing to him in those days. He was beginning to doze when the elevator door opened and the doctor walked out, followed by the boy's father. They were laughing. This made the boy cry again and he rushed up to hug the two men.

"Bullshit? Is that what he said?" Doctor Binatti asked, and laughed even harder, leaning on the elevator door.

"Boolsheet," Milad said. "He open up his eyes and seen the priest putting oil on his head, and he said 'Boolsheet' and went right back asleep." Laughing, he picked his son up and hugged him. "You kiss Doctor Binatti's hand," he said, "because himself he stop the bleeding." The boy tried, but the doctor stuck his hands

in his coat pockets and said, "Boolsheet." Then the boy said "Enwaddyelse?" in a tone of mock impatience, and the three of them stood laughing in front of the open elevator.

With administration of the Last Sacrament, Uncle E's long silence had begun. The next day there was an operation, and Doctor Binatti removed part of the stomach. During the whole of his hospital recovery Uncle E spoke to no one, answering questions with a tired nod of his head for yes or a click of his tongue for no. At home he did not go back to work, but stayed in his room, in his bed. Guests who came all the way from Cleveland or Detroit to see him sat in his bedroom talking among themselves, or simply staring at the bed. And propped up by pillows, he would stare back at them. Soon they would stand up and go into the living room, saying to Milad, "That is not like Elias at all. He has lost weight. His face is all eyes."

Doctor Binatti had specialists come over, but they could find nothing wrong with the throat or the tongue. They wheeled him back to the hospital for x rays, and the x rays showed nothing, and they brought him home again. And still he was silent. So Milad and the doctor tried trickery. They surprised the old man by sending for people he had not seen in years, Aunt Anissa from New York, Danny the butcher from the old store on Congress Street in Detroit. But he merely wept and hugged the visitors and kissed them on the neck. They tried funny stories, and he smiled at them, silently. Milad even woke him in the middle of a deep sleep. But this, too, failed for the old man opened his eyes and calmly waited for Milad to say something. And realizing that Milad had nothing to say, he closed his eyes and went back to sleep. "It is not depression," Doctor Binatti had finally said, "it is goddamn stubbornness."

*

The boy ladles the oatmeal into a bowl and pours milk over it. Through the kitchen doorway he can hear the grind and ring of the cash register. Customers, he thinks. His father will want him to come down soon and help out. Beyond the wall the toilet flushes, roaring and sucking. The boy sticks a spoon in the oatmeal.

Uncle E is sitting up in bed when the boy nudges the door open and enters, the bowl in both hands. The old man smiles his thanks and begins to eat, but the boy does not leave. He stands at a corner of the bed, his dark eyes scheming as they scan the photographs and holy pictures on the wall. A few moments pass, and Uncle E smiles again, this time a brief, impatient smile that means his nephew should leave now. The boy knows that smile well, but he waits still a moment more before leaving. Closing the door behind him, he hurries to the kitchen and runs downstairs to the store. His father is making change for a customer. When he finishes, he turns to his son.

"Put the soup up."

"Feel my forehead, Baba," the boy asks in Arabic.

"You sick?"

"I don't know."

Milad puts his lips to the boy's forehead. He feels that it is, perhaps, just a little warm. "Go upstairs, get in bed," he says in Arabic.

The boy trudges to the stairs and climbs slowly until he reaches the top. Then he rushes to his uncle's room, enters, and sits in a chair at the foot of the bed. The old man, napping after his breakfast, is startled and sits up. But the boy says nothing. He stares at his uncle, looks him full in the eyes from his place at the end of the long bed. The old man waits, then lays his head back against the pillows and gazes at the ceiling. The boy looks up there too. There is a small crack and, in a corner, a water stain. There is nothing else.

Uncle E pats the bed with the flat of his hand, another signal that he would like to be alone. But the boy does not leave. He puts his feet on the rung of the chair and traces with his eyes the flowered pattern of the pillowcases. The old man releases a great breath of air and seems to fall asleep. Outside the curtained window pigeons mutter in high, throaty voices on the flat roof of the bar next door. That, and his uncle's soft snores lull the boy, and the sound of his own deep breathing soon falls into the rhythm of the room's quiet murmur. He sleeps uneasily in the chair, dreams he is falling, and wakes with a shudder to catch himself, safe, still seated. Uncle E raises his head and, with one eye open, sees that the boy is still there. He makes a terrible face, but it seems to plead more than threaten, and the boy turns to the wall. Time passes quickly, for soon the boy is hungry. He has been studying the face on the pillows, the large nose with its deep black nostrils, white hair in the ears; but now he is hungry, and he goes into the kitchen.

When he returns, with a poached egg on toast for his uncle and a liverwurst sandwich for himself, the old man is sitting up and seems, by his half-smile, in a better mood. As they eat, the uncle watches his nephew, waiting for him to say something. But he says nothing. The boy clears his throat once while swallowing, but nothing follows. There is only the chewing and the silence and the pigeons outside. The man cannot eat, and the boy finishes only part of his sandwich.

It is beginning to get dark in the apartment. The boy puts the plates and the oatmeal bowl in the kitchen sink, goes into the bathroom, and turns on the light. There are a few drops of blood on the lip of the toilet bowl. He feels a pain, sharp and tight in his stomach, and he runs into the bedroom and finds the light switch. As the overhead light snaps on, the old man sits up and throws a pillow at the boy. "Uncle E!" the boy shouts, and the flowered pillow strikes him in the chest and knocks him

backward against the door. He tosses the pillow aside and stands glaring into his uncle's eyes. Then slowly, deliberately, he turns to one side and spits. Nothing comes from his mouth, only the sound.

The old man leans forward. "Enwaddyelse?" he asks sharply, and his voice is high-pitched and full of breath.

They continue to stare at each other, uncle and nephew, and the boy trembles as though with fever, but he says nothing. He nears the bed, takes his uncle's hand and kisses it. "We will eat pigeons tonight," he says, and his uncle nods.

Less than a month later the boy will stand in the sunshine of the cemetery, weeping with the other men, wailing his uncle's name. But he does not join the others in the throwing of flowers, when that time comes, not at this funeral nor at any of the other many funerals he will attend: his father's when cancer takes him, that of a teacher he loved in high school, the sad and painful funeral for Doctor Binatti, the military funeral for his own first son. Instead he will weep by the grave, as each is opened with time, and then return home. The next day he opens his supermarket, business as usual, working behind the butcher counter, marking prices on white wrapping paper. And when he has added everything up he asks the customer, "And what else?" And the customer thanks him, saying that there is nothing else.

Through and Through

Back when I was first on the lam from the Jackie Kennedy murder (the Toledo beer baron, not the other one) I spent some time in Damascus, Syria. There, not far from the house where my father grew up, is a street called Straight. *National Geographic* says it's the oldest continually inhabited street in the world – more than five thousand years old – and my uncle took a day off work to show it to me. He was a bricklayer, helping to put up the new (then, in 1933) church commemorating the spot where Saint Paul was supposedly knocked from his horse and blinded by the light of Jesus. I remember how my uncle tried to put his arm in my arm and walk me along like a girl. I'd been warned they did that over there, men even holding hands. All pretty harmless, but I shrugged him off anyway. Twenty-two and on the lam, I'd just as soon keep my hands free.

(Yes, we really did say "On the lam" – the movies got that from us, not the other way around.)

It was about noon when we reached Straight Street and the *souk* stalls were crowded. A metal framework stretched building to building over the street, supporting sheets of canvas that protected from the sun and wind, but which also trapped clouds of yellow dust that hung in the air as thick as cigar smoke back in the old Devon Club on a Saturday night.

Well, there I was, twenty-two, and I remember trying to grasp the whole five thousand years, imagining all the sweat, blood, and urine spilled on this one piece of ground, the semen and the spit and the tears. Not long ago the *National Enquirer* had an insert that I cut out and put in my wallet; it says that, per minute, a human being at rest sheds more than a hundred thousand microscopic particles of flaked off flesh, saliva, lint, sodium, dandruff, dead mouth tissue. Per minute. At rest. A slight head movement, and the number jumps to five hundred thousand particles. Five million when you walk real slow. Thirty million before you even get going good.

Five thousand years. Even now I try to grasp it. What the hell was I standing on?

*

Today, fifty-two years later, I am standing at a motel window with a view of a storage tank off Ohio Route 12, on the road to Toledo. It is night. There are crowds outside, people selling T-shirts and photographs of the storage tank, which is orange in the vapor lights. The *Review Times* says it is filled with soybean oil. I have prayed to Saint Helen, who first recovered the True Cross, and to Saint Anthony of Padua, finder of lost things. I am not drinking. At first I saw only rust streaks and flaked paint, not even a pattern. The diagrams published in *Time* magazine didn't help me any, even with these bifocals. I tried polarized sunglasses, and they were no help. I wished for those red-and-green lenses from the 3-D movies of the fifties. Then my eyes started playing tricks on me.

I suffer from poor eyesight. And from an ache in my hip. The doctor will probably say it is rheumatism. (But at night, alone in bed, I sometimes watch him shake his head and say cancer.) Only six of my own teeth remain in my mouth, and all six of them hurt. And I have gas. Everything I eat gives me gas. Which is particles that

shoot out of you. Most people don't know that. Keep your nose clean, we used to say. We didn't know what we were saying.

I try opera glasses, but all they do is give size to what I think I see. The hard rainbow edges hurt my eyes and confuse me, all of it trembling because my hand won't hold still. In my other hand I hold the microphone to a portable cassette tape recorder. I tested it, and I sound just like me, whispering. Only younger. I even have an accent again, like when I was a kid, whispering.

In 1927, in the Detroit Pick-Fort Selby Hotel, Thomas "Yonnie" Licavoli, who was six feet tall and weighed 210 pounds and who never in his life talked above a whisper, told the Big Guy himself, Al Capone, "Stay the hell out of Detroit. It's my territory." The Big Guy agreed, and Yonnie's name — which is everything in this business — was made. At the time he was waiting for the Purple and Little Navy gangs to finish each other off in the war they were having. The famous Collingwood Avenue Massacre was what finally ended the war. That, and the ten-storey death leap of a beautiful young woman, a known companion to one of the Purples. It seems that the *Detroit Free Press* somehow discovered that what the police were calling a suicide victim happened to've been bound and gagged at the time of death. Detroit put up its hackles, and things got too hot too fast, even for Yonnie Licavoli. It was right about then that Jacob "Firetop" Sulkin made all those trips to Detroit he bragged about later, convincing Yonnie and his gang to set up in Toledo. The only problem, he told them, would be a minor one, name of Jackie Kennedy.

Was he in with the dicks? Yonnie wanted to know. In solid, Firetop said. And with the Irish politicians, too. But Kennedy's only real connections were with Egan's Rats out of St. Louis. And Yonnie Licavoli knew all about them, their shooter with the smoked glasses,

name of Browning. Yonnie was from St. Louis himself, dropped out of the Christian Brothers college there.

Me, my only school was what we called the College of Hard Knocks. My father enrolled me. He used to brag about how he'd lifted a sliver of the True Cross off a Turk who tried selling it to him. He always kept it wrapped in adhesive and slung around his neck on a string. He told people that if he ever lost it, he'd lose all his luck.

Back when I was about twelve or so I figured I'd need all the luck I could get. It took some doing, but I was already a good sneak. I managed to get it off him without his ever knowing what happened to it. Not long after that I said good riddance to my father's house and made it through Ellis Island in 1921, just under the wire of the Quota Act. Lucky me.

I traveled with "relatives" from my village, and we wound up running a produce market in Toledo's North End. By that time word reached me that I'd left none too soon—it seemed my father's health was declining, and his feed and grain business wasn't feeling so well either.

Like most of my people, these "relatives" I worked for were what was called industrious, but what I called penny scratchers. The North End was a clannish neighborhood—Little Syria—and in no time I'd developed a name for myself as something of a pickpocket. I took this as a compliment—I was a kid, what did I know?—but it was embarrassing to my adopted family who were straight shooters, doing their best by sending me to Catholic school and finding me work afterward (although it wasn't in school or in work but by playing hooky at the movies that I learned to speak English without an accent). So I moved on and ended up working on Canton Avenue in old Saint Patrick's Parish at the B and L Confectionery—a candy store where, on the QT, a Catholic could get himself a pail of beer after

mass. The beer was supplied by Jackie Kennedy, who wore pearl gray spats and a pinky ring. He was twenty-four years old and handsome and singing a love song to his sweetheart when they killed him. They put eleven holes in him. Jacob "Firetop" Sulkin supplied the roscoes. I was the fingerman.

We really called a pistol a roscoe. It sounds funny now, after so many movies. It was at the B and L that I first learned to talk like that. I met Firetop there, and through him I got to know "Chalky Red" Yaranowsky and "Yonnie" Licavoli and "Wop" English and the rest. We all really did use those nicknames. Firetop because of his red hair and Chalky Red because of his complexion and Joe English the Wop because his true name was Serifina Sinatra. There was even a Buster and a Blackjack in the old Licavoli Gang. Just like the movies. They called me "Dip." Somebody spread around a lie about me that I picked pockets. It was a bad name and a reputation I didn't deserve, as it was a knack I rarely used anymore, and only when I was desperate. Myself, I'd've settled for something like "The Shadow" or even "Sneaky Pete" (my name was once Peter, in Arabic, Boutros) but Dip was what stuck because the big shots, Yonnie and Firetop, made it stick, and there wasn't much I could do about it. Al Capone said once that there's nothing lower than a dip. (Well, "Rummy" would've been worse, which was why I did most of my drinking on the sly.) Capone himself never stood for being called "Scarface"—he preferred "Snorky," which in those days we used to mean a snappy dresser. But nobody called him that, either. I saw him only once, on an elevator in Cleveland. He looked thick more than fat, back then in 1930, and on the short side, yet I could tell right off why everybody called him "The Big Guy." His reputation shone off him like a glow, like the golden light you see in holy cards. The Big Guy. He wore a

cream fedora with the brim snapped down on the left to shadow the double razor scars. He nodded to me. Hasty, like somebody who didn't like to waste his time. Then one of his boys gave me the thumbs out sign, and I got off at the next floor.

For me it was pretty clear that if I ever did want a respected name, I'd have to work for it. So when Firetop called – I already knew what for – I was quick to be of service.

I uncovered Jackie Kennedy at a cottage over in Point Place, near Toledo. It took a sneak with talent to find and finger him. I learned that there was only one bodyguard, who was mostly kept busy playing babysitter to Jackie's four-year-old son. The time was right, I figured, even though Firetop wasn't around and Yonnie was in Detroit for his father-in-law's funeral. Chalky Red couldn't make it either, but his Ford V-8 did. And me in it, sitting behind the wheel.

When the boys got out, they found Jackie strolling hand in hand with Audrey Rawls, a beauty contest winner. He was singing "Love in the Moonlight" to her, like in a movie. Afterward some of the papers called her the "Tiger Woman" because they figured her to be the Judas. But she wasn't involved at all. I watched through the windscreen as Wop and Magnine shoved Miss Rawls out of the way and emptied both their .38 revolvers. One round blew off his watch. The other eleven were what coroners list as "through and through" – in then right out the other side; clean, but they leave less evidence. Kennedy was tall and muscular and so strong his feet did the Jackson Shuffle for a full minute after he went down. That happened on July the 7th, 1933, a Friday.

Today is also a Friday – October the 3rd, 1986. My present name is John Doe. I deny all and any other appellations, true names, nicknames, monikers, handles or

tags. I am seventy-four years old, and this is my deposition, which I give freely and without coercion or duress, without hope of reward or recompense.

The names I name have not been changed. Harry "Chalky Red" Yaranowsky is a real name. So is Jacob "Firetop" Sulkin. So is Thomas "Yonnie" Licavoli. They are as dead as Jackie Kennedy. But they have not disappeared. They are in the *Toledo Blade*, the *Detroit News*, the *Cleveland Plain Dealer*, the *New York Times*. Me, I am in none of them. I got away. My current whereabouts are known only to the four walls of this room.

Until nine months ago my address was the same as that of my latest place of business, the English Language newsstand, mezzanine, St. Georges Hotel, Beirut, in what, as far as I know, is still being called Lebanon; my more recent names and addresses are too numerous to list. My father has been deceased for over sixty years; I didn't have a mother that I could remember. I never married, and currently I cannot be found.

*

Because they were so well known, Yonnie and Firetop couldn't get away after the murder. But they had the lawyers and the alibis. Now all they had to do was keep their mouths shut. Which they did until the Toledo cops sent to Detroit for a pair of dicks who specialized in extracting information. For some reason the *Toledo Blade* called these two the Clarke brothers, which anybody who knew anything knew wasn't their real name. But most people don't know anything. Most people think things like this happened only in the movies. But they should believe what they see in gangster movies. Who do they think made the movies? Anyway, the Clarkes figured Firetop to be the soft one, since he bragged so much. One session with him lasted from after supper one night until 2:30 the next morning. His ribs were cracked and he couldn't walk because his groin hurt so.

Me, I'm hearing all this and I figure he'll spill in no time. Anybody would've. So if ever there was a time to take a fade, this was it.

I remember one night I'd sneaked out to eat at a place down the road from Toledo in New Regal, Ohio. (The place still has a reputation for the best ribs around. I ate there two nights ago. Some things, like food, never change.) So there I was, fifty-some years ago, adjusting the napkin at my neck, the whole time thinking should I blow town or the whole midwest—in other words, how long is the long arm of the law?—when I happened to touch the lump of the True Cross where I kept it beneath my shirt. If anybody ever needed direction, it was me there and then. So I asked. Nothing. Okay. I started eating my ribs. Then, an instant later, I had my answer. There was a voice, not in my ears exactly, more like inside my head, telling me what to do.

I'd been an altar boy, but unlike most I took it seriously. I have always considered myself a spiritual person. To this day I believe that God speaks to us, and not just on the road to the holy city of Damascus, but on the road to Toledo, Ohio, too.

What the voice said was this: Do not blow town, My child. Blow the whole country.

*

Beirut would have been like heaven except that on the way there I discovered that my piece of the True Cross had been lifted from me. I was in New York Harbor, undressing in my cabin, when I felt, then looked and saw that it wasn't there. The last place I'd had my shirt off was in my flat above the B and L. So it had to still be in Toledo. But it was too late to go back. And too hot—Yonnie's trial had already begun. Being on the lam is like swimming underwater in the movies. You surface for air, see the patrol boat closing in behind you, and you go down again, deeper this time.

I had a couple of drinks, and after a while I said to

myself Okay, it doesn't have to be the one great tragedy of your life. Go on, then, and make your own luck. I was surprised at how cocky I sounded. Besides, word had it that Lebanon, if not heaven, was a lot like home. A handful of family syndicates ran the whole place with defined territories, bosses, and soldiers. Like the States, except it was called politics. Sure, vice was pretty much legal, gambling and prostitution, but there was the black market. And plenty of business from the hashish growers in Baalbek north of Beirut. Beirut Harbor itself was a conduit between the Turkish poppy fields and Marseilles.

Unfortunately, the luck I ended up making for myself over there wasn't too good, and before long I developed a liking for *arraq* (which is similar to absinthe, and because of that is illegal in the States to this day), but not so much that I got a name for it. The depression ended in the States and in Europe, but in the Middle East it lingered on into the war. Later, working with the *heil* Hitler Vichy government was like doing business with the Boy Scouts. So our cheers were real when the Free French Senegalese marched into Martyr's Square to liberate us, their faces as black and shiny as their boots. After the boys in Italy finally did Benito (long overdue), the Mediterranean shipping lanes reopened and business started booming again.

The Bourj Plaza educated me. At one time I could speak French, Arabic, and get by in Greek and German. When I used to change money in the Ashrifiyeh District, the Armenians thought I was one of them. But I've lost all that now, all of it faded.

I worked on the up-and-up at hotel newsstands, and for real as a kind of errand boy for couriers who needed interpreting. In other words, one step above a dip. What I was called was *Il Amerikain* because my Arabic had developed an accent. You might say I didn't really have a name. Still, it became a life. I almost got married once

but I sobered up and decided not to. There were even times luck came my way, as they say in the movies, and for a while I'd be what anybody'd call happy. *Arraq* stayed cheap, and even under the Boy Scouts the prostitute district remained open in Bourj Plaza, just behind the Gendarmerie. It was a life. If I had no name, at least I could say I was hanging on to the fringe, anyway, of the kind of work where a man might some day make a name. And, unlike Yonnie and Firetop, I was free.

Firetop served thirty years for his part in the Jackie Kennedy murder. He was granted parole in 1965, on his seventy-fifth birthday. Word reached me that he'd turned sour. Nobody feared him, calling him "Schmuck" to his face. He had to be straitjacketed, finally, and sent to the Toledo State Hospital for the mentally ill. He died there in 1971.

I took the news hard. It was, as they used to say in the movies, like losing a part of myself.

Beirut had a dozen or more picture shows called cinemas, and for a while I went to every American movie. In 1971 I saw *Easy Rider* dubbed in Arabic and subtitled in French. It frightened me. I was fifty-nine years old.

For me, the boom years – such as they were – ended with the Lebanese civil war. People got so they couldn't trust their own cousins, much less Il Amerikain. When the Syrians marched in with their half-a-goosestep clomp, it was like the Boy Scouts all over again. Car bombs went off sometimes twice a day, and I found myself reduced to working the crowds that gathered afterward. A dip.

Then, not long ago, I read in *Time,* in an article on organized crime, that Yonnie Licavoli was dead. Had been dead for over a dozen years. Nobody'd sent word. There was nobody left to send word. I closed the magazine and rolled it tight. I walked away from the newsstand without even bothering to lock up. The bottle of

arraq sat uncorked on the counter. I left it there to evaporate. I began walking and I kept on walking, all the time twisting and choking the magazine. Those steps were the beginning of my journey back to Toledo.

*

Thomas "Yonnie" Licavoli, while an inmate of the Ohio State Penitentiary, had been granted two first place awards in international stamp collectors' exhibits. He also won recognition for fifty songs he wrote under the name Tommy Thomas. Over the years three different wardens lost their jobs for allowing him special treatment. So for Yonnie, too, it had become a life. When he was sixty-seven years old he pleaded for release. "I have a daughter who was born three months before I came to prison," he wrote the governor. "Now she is married, with two lovely girls and a little boy of her own, and none of them have ever seen me except behind bars. My first-born daughter was killed, along with my father, while they were on their way to visit me one day." The letter is public record. The only word that reaches me anymore is public record.

Yonnie Licavoli was released after serving thirty-seven years, one month, and twenty-seven days. And he died less than two years later. His obit made the *New York Times*. The FBI attended the funeral in Detroit. A sixty-car procession followed the hearse.

Now they are all gone – Wop English, Chalky Red, Blackjack, Pimp Bruno, Buster Lupica. Johnny Magnine, like me, was never found. Word had it he died in Akron back in '35. A week ago I stopped there on my way back to check it out. Nobody knew. He was the other triggerman, but the memory of him had faded completely. Through and through. For the first time in fifty-two years I felt free to surface. What was left of me.

It was while I was on my way back from Akron, almost to Toledo, that I read about the face of Jesus on a water tower.

Except that when I got here it turned out to be this soybean oil storage tank, and maybe it's the light or something reflecting on the rust and the paint that edges the rust, but whole crowds are seeing something there. I tried, and for the briefest instant I thought I saw something, too. Yet what I saw—if I saw it—was nothing like the Image outlined in *Time*. What I saw had on a hat, a fedora, with the brim snapped down to hide the left cheek. Then the light began to hurt my eyes and the Image receded once more to rust stains and peeling paint and crowds of people looking. All of them faders. You'd think He wouldn't waste His time on faders. On sodium and lint and dead tissue that flakes away with every motion. Standing still even, I feel myself changing. The light blinds me the more I stare. I pull the drapes against it.

There's nothing left in Toledo, not after all this time. I can see that now. Now what I want to see is how much of me will be left when I get there, and what I'll be.